"I've been looking for you ever since Irena left."

Irena. Obviously Irena had left the fires still burning and he'd come to Jade to put them out....

"Let go of me! I don't *want* you."

Zan touched the hollow of her neck. "Your pulse is going crazy," he murmured thickly. "Your body wants me, Jade."

"Well, it's been outvoted," she said clearly, her eyes blazing.

His hand traced slowly down to her breast, a burning touch that nearly melted her resolve. "I think I could change your mind." He was laughing softly, his hand gliding to her back to urge her toward him.

She gave a sharp cry and cursed herself for being every kind of fool. She would *not* be a stand-in for Irena!

PEGGY NICHOLSON

the darling jade

Harlequin Books

TORONTO • NEW YORK • LONDON
AMSTERDAM • PARIS • SYDNEY • HAMBURG
STOCKHOLM • ATHENS • TOKYO • MILAN

Harlequin Presents first edition October 1984
ISBN 0-373-10732-3

Original hardcover edition published in 1984
by Mills & Boon Limited

CHAPTER ONE

PLANTS thrive on conversation, and the potted herbs on the kitchen windowsill were flourishing. 'I have a feeling,' Jade told the chives, 'that today will be special. It's going to be one of those days when nothing can go wrong.' She studied the square of deep violet sky beyond the tender greens. Deep violet, but fading fast—it would dawn clear. And it would dawn without her, if she didn't hurry. The tea kettle whistled.

Topping off the thermos, she set it on the table by her paintbox and watercolour block, and paused to check her wrist watch. Nearly four-forty, damn it! Her extra ten minutes in bed had stretched to twenty somehow. There was no time for breakfast, if she wanted to beat the sun to the beach. Grabbing an apple from the bowl on the counter, she found her keys and hustled out of the door, her arms full of gear and a smile in her green eyes.

And just what would Fred think when he discovered she had a penchant for painting seascapes at dawn? Jade wondered, as she scampered down the stairs. In their two years of teaching together, he'd never seen that darker side of her nature, had he? It was scarcely in evidence in the cold New England winters, when she played the staid, responsible teacher of art in a private high school. And by summer, when she shed that role to become the manic painter, drunk on early light and her own freedom, he was far away in Greece, digging earnestly through the dirt for shards of pottery and bits of metal. Well, he would know the worst of her very soon—next week, in fact. No doubt there were surprises in store for her as well.

Shutting the front door behind her, Jade crossed the

porch and tiptoed down the steps. She winced as they creaked ferociously, probably woke half the neighbourhood. She would have to fix that in the fall when they returned. She laughed softly. Or maybe next year. Her list of projects seemed to grow with each passing month, rather than shrink. Home ownership was a mixed blessing, she was finding. But she glanced back at her two-storey Victorian cottage with pride before turning to scan the sky in the east.

It was paler now, but she was still ahead of the sun. She stepped out into the dark street, sniffing the soft, warm air of early June. Summer in Newport, Rhode Island—could anything be sweeter? It would almost be a shame to miss it, after pining for lilac and beach roses, green trees and warm seas all winter long. But then Greece would have its charms too, she assured herself. And it was too late for second thoughts now.

Too late—and where had she last parked the bug? Jade peered along the row of parked cars that lined her street. She hadn't driven it in three days, not since her insurance had lapsed. Spotting a battered tan bumper beyond a dark Ford, she hurried up the street, her wide mouth curved in a smile. The choices you had to make when you were broke! She threw open the VW's door, tossed her painting kit behind the seat, and slipped her long, bare legs beneath the steering wheel.

And yet it had seemed a reasonable, even fitting, choice—trading her car insurance money for an airline ticket to Greece. That's me, she thought, throwing caution to the winds and taking a flyer! Her heart-shaped face flickered in a brief frown as the thought formed. No, that wasn't exactly right. The first half of the thought *was* true; she was reckless and impulsive. She had that from her mother—as she had been brutally reminded a few months ago. But dear solid, sensible Fred could hardly be considered a flyer. He'd been patiently and cheerfully waiting for her to come to her senses for three years now.

If anyone was taking a flyer, it was him in marrying her! She edged the bug out of its place and into the street. Well, he'd not regret it. Her reversal might have been sudden, but it was wholehearted. She glanced at the sky again. In the meantime, I've got a week to myself in which to paint, and a dawn to catch. Get moving, girl! She stepped on the gas.

Within a few blocks, the close-packed shingle and clapboard houses of a Victorian working class gave way to thick, sheltering hedges and high granite walls, as Jade skirted the back of the mansion district. Beyond the walls, ornate rooflines and fanciful towers loomed dark against the cobalt sky, then vanished behind her. But this morning she had no time to admire the summer cottages. Fabulous relics of Newport's gilded age, the fairy-castle monuments to the pre-income tax empires of Vanderbilts and Astors merely blocked her view. She would have to drive further out along the point to watch the sun rise over the ocean.

As Jade picked a winding route south to the sea, pruned trees and stone walls gave way to wind-blasted scrubby woods cut by granite ridges. The rough lonely spine of the point that sheltered Newport harbour from the Atlantic was deserted at this hour, and she could choose her own speed on the corkscrew roads. The little car hummed along, bouncing through the potholes and swaying wide on the curves as the thickets faded from green-black to emerald.

Jade rolled down her car window and leaned out to feel the wind on her face. Wisps of long hair escaped the clasp at her neck to wave in the salt breeze and then curl damply on her cheeks and shoulders. She could smell the ocean now, and flowers. The scents roused her stomach and she groped for the apple, but after taking a bite, she wrinkled her nose—mushy! Passing it to her left hand, she held it poised above the rushing road for a second, then lobbed it skyward. She stole a glance back to watch it bomb into the bushes, red into deep green, and grinned. Some early-rising rabbit would be in ecstasy, no doubt.

Her stomach muttered in sullen envy, and she smiled again. Too late now. It would just have to settle for the coffee in her thermos. And even that would have to wait till she'd finished her first painting. The light changed too quickly in that first half-hour of sunrise to pause for an instant. There wouldn't be time to pre-mix her colours, as it was. The wind whipped a curl into her teeth and she brushed it back impatiently. *Hurry!*

Swooping over a hill, she flushed a pheasant, missed him by inches as he took off with a metallic squawk, in a flurry of copper. Jade laughed in sheer delight. She felt reckless and alive in her race with the sun, her senses as vivid and eager as if she'd just been born this morning. She laughed again.

And morning it nearly was. Jade flicked off the headlights. No need for them now in the pearly light. Above the beach scrub, the sea mist was tinged now with expectant rose. She glanced at her watch. But you haven't won yet, she told the sun, putting her foot to the floor. Wait just one minute and I'll catch you yet! The bug leaped ahead.

Wheeling around a tight corner, she bore down on a stop sign at a crossroads—not much further now. She slowed, glanced both ways, then jumped the stop sign, smiling as she thought of Fred, who would stop at a broken red light in the middle of the Sahara at three a.m., and would probably stay put till someone fixed it. But Fred wasn't here to be shocked. There was no one for miles around, just her and the coming sun in a world smelling of honeysuckle and seaweed.

The bug took the last hill, hummed down to the narrow road's junction with the ocean drive. Jade slowed the car, flicked her eyes to left and right, scanning the open road beyond the clump of trees at the corner. Not a car in sight, and no need to stop. She went over the stop sign smoothly, then pulled out to the left, her eyes on the brightening sky.

'Oh!'

As she started the turn, something large bobbed before her. The shape dodged to the right-reached, twisting, for the bumper. Rubber screamed and slipped on damp pavement as she braked, didn't drown out the thump as the car connected and the shape flew aside. And then there was nothing—just the soft hush of the ocean and sunlight.

'Oh, my God!' Jade watched a hand reach out before her to turn off the engine. The keys tinkled as her fingers shook. There was no road before her, she noticed dimly. The car tilted forward, its front wheels in the weeds, facing the ditch. How had she got here?

And where was he? 'Oh, my God!' Fumbling at the door, she hammered on it as the catch resisted, then gave, and half fell into the road. Where was he? She stared around blindly, her breath loud in the silence. Nothing. She couldn't have imagined it, could she? No, she shook her head dazedly, that half-glimpsed shape had been human, that thump too real. Where had he come from? And where had he gone?

The thought hit her and she stooped to stare beneath the car, her teeth biting into her lip. 'Oh, my *God*!'

The sound was faint, halfway between a snort and a laugh. 'No such luck, girl. I'm over here.'

'*Oh!*' She whirled.

Twenty feet behind the car a man knelt in the weeds, his right arm cradled in his left, his eyes on her face. 'Oh.' She returned his stare, feeling relief surge through her in a sickening rush. The ground tilted strangely as she wobbled towards him, his odd light eyes holding her wide green ones.

'Sit down before you fall down,' he commanded.

Jade knelt before him, dizzy with gratitude, and found she had to look up to meet his eyes.

Tears gleamed in the edges of his thick gold lashes. The heavy gold eyebrows were clenched in a frown of concentration, as if all his energy was focussed outward in the laser beam of the pale grey eyes. 'Got a licence to hunt with that thing?' he asked.

'What?'

Beads of sweat gleamed in the golden pelt across his wide chest, in the curling hairs along the muscular arm he held so carefully. This time the low voice had an edge to it. 'I said, do you have a licence to hunt with that car, sweetheart? They didn't tell me it was open season on runners in Rhode Island.'

'I—it isn't.' Jade shook her head miserably, trying to collect her wits. If he'd just be quiet a minute. 'Are you all right?'

'And is your face always green, or is this—'

'Will you shut up and listen to me!' She snapped, surprising them both into silence. She reached for his arm. 'How is your—'

'Uh!' he flinched away, hugging the arm closer. 'Don't touch, thanks! You've done enough for one day. We'll leave this to the doctors, shall we?'

Jade bit her lip. 'Of course—stupid of me. I'll go call an ambulance, right now.' She bounced to her feet, then swayed as the world darkened around her.

'Steady!' A warm hand clamped around her calf, the hard fingers nearly encircling her slim leg. She froze, waiting for her vision to clear, all her senses focussed on those warm fingers.

The hand squeezed slightly, slid slowly down her calf and then dropped away. She could see first his eyes and then his face now as the faintness passed. 'Slow down, girl.' He smiled tightly and reached to cradle his right arm again. 'You don't drive away from the scene of an accident, remember? At least, not till I get your licence plate numbers.'

'You think I'd—'

'I don't think anything,' he cut in irritably, 'but you're not leaving.' He grunted and began to stand.

'Oh, *wait*!' Jade put out her hands, then stopped, afraid to quite touch him. She hovered before him like a basketball guard, waiting for him to fall, as he rose stiffly between her hands and kept on rising. He straightened and she found herself blinking at his hard furry chest. She took a step backwards, looking up. 'You shouldn't move,' she protested.

White teeth showed in what passed for a smile. 'I'll be damned if I'll just sit there in the briars all day! Do you know where there's a hospital?'

'Yes, but what about leaving your scene of the accident?'

He scowled around, glanced at the stop sign, then down at her, his grey eyes hard with pain. 'It's pretty clear-cut, isn't it? You never stopped. You admit you jumped the sign and hit me, don't you?'

'Yes,' she gulped. 'I'm so sorry!'

'Me too,' he said dryly. 'But we can settle that later.' He stepped forward haltingly, nodded in grim satisfaction, and took another step.

'Are—are you sure you should walk?'

His teeth flashed again. 'Want to try carrying me?' he asked rhetorically, limping stiffly towards her car. 'I'm sore, but it's just the arm that really hurts. I fended off with it, and that's all you hit as you came around.' He scowled. 'It would be the right one, wouldn't you know!' He inspected her car contemptuously, and as she opened the door for him, he shook his head. 'I do choose my accidents, don't I?' he said wryly. 'Run down by a beautiful, green-faced redhead in a decrepit VW. I guess I'm lucky you don't drive a Cadillac.'

'Do you always talk so much, or are you just in shock?' Jade scowled at him.

He sat down stiffly in the seat, stared glumly at his long, muscular legs yet to be folded inside. 'It's just stark terror, sweetheart. You will stop at all the stop signs, just to please me?'

She glared at his teasing male face, noticed the muscles knotted tight at the jawline, the teeth clamped shut once the jeering words were out, and nodded humbly. She shut his door gently. She should be grateful he wasn't cursing her, after all.

The car was full of him, she discovered, when she climbed in. Her hand grazed his hard thigh as she shifted into reverse and backed them on to the road. She tried not to flinch as her knuckles brushed the curly blond hair along his leg again, and then again as she shifted into second.

He leaned back in the seat and shut his eyes, smiling tightly. 'We'll just have to enjoy it, sweetheart,' he told her quietly, the low voice amused. 'There's no place left for me to go.'

Gritting her teeth, Jade shifted to third. 'My pleasure,' she said icily. She *would* have to run down a wise-guy! 'And I'm not a redhead, by the way.'

'Oh?' The golden brows clenched as the car jounced through a pothole.

'I'm sorry!'

'Sure . . . What . . . do you call it, then?' he asked breathlessly.

'Auburn, when it's this dark.'

'Whatever you say, lady. Just keep your eyes on the stop signs, and don't ever cut it.' The gold lashes squeezed tight, then eased again as if he were willing his face to relax. He breathed deeply and slowly, as if he were counting each breath.

Jade stared blindly at the beautiful morning outside her windshield as the little car whirred along the drive. Beyond the mansions on the rocks, the sun was well up, burning off the sea mist, turning the grey dawn Atlantic to morning blue. He'd won their race, slid up the sky, smug and serene, while she bagged her runner. Hubris, that was what Fred and his Greeks would call it, to race the sun. The gods didn't tolerate that kind of pride and nonsense for long, did they?

Jade bit her lip. Well, they'd brought her down quickly enough. Or she'd brought herself down, rather. To drive without insurance—what dim-witted folly! And then to jump stop signs! She deserved everything that was coming to her, and more. The only mercy was that she hadn't killed the man.

Though maybe she should have, she thought ruefully. Dead men tell no tales, after all. She flicked a glance at the shuttered face beside her, and smiled wryly. Nope, not a chance. She was lucky she hadn't broken her car, as it was. He was large.

She stole another look at his profile as they turned off the drive and on to Bellevue Avenue. It was an interesting face. Not so handsome as Fred's, she thought quickly, but arresting, with its hard, flat planes meeting in sharp angles, the long, carved lips, and the hint of a cleft in the square chin. His straight nose hooked slightly at the top, as if he'd broken it once upon a time . . . Rather a hard face, you might say, but then that first impression of toughness was softened by the loose fall of honey-dark blond hair across his brow. And the thick lashes brushing his cheeks seemed to give it the lie— until you remembered that those closed eyes were not the usual blue, but the grey of granite, or polished steel. An interesting face . . .

And somehow familiar. Frowning suddenly, Jade turned back to the road. Jack? Why should . . . how could that pain-bleak face remind her of foxy, laughing, despicable Jack? Her hands clenched on the wheel. She hadn't let herself think of Jack in months—and didn't mean to now. No, there was no resemblance. None at all.

She slowed down smoothly as they encountered traffic, grazed his thigh as she shifted to third. She scanned his doubled legs with their crisp haze of curly gold. Going by their thick muscularity, it looked as if he'd been running for quite some time. You didn't get legs like that in a week, or even a month, of jogging. And he must lift weights as well, she thought, glancing at his arms, or else do manual labour. He was a wholehearted jock of some sort, without a doubt.

'When do we get there?'

Jade jumped guiltily and looked up at his face, her clear skin flaming. But his eyes were still shut, thank heavens. 'Just a few more blocks, now . . . Does it hurt?'

He didn't bother to answer that, but his lips twitched. Slowly they tightened to form a hard line again.

She pulled up to the emergency room door at the rear of the hospital, and stopped the VW. 'You'd better get out here. I'll park the car.'

The ice-grey eyes snapped open, inspected her face gravely. 'No, thanks. I'll walk with you, I think,' he said crisply.

Jade shrugged, flushing angrily as she found a parking place. Did he really think she'd dump him and run? On the other hand, in the age of million-dollar lawsuits, didn't hitting and running have its own dreadful kind of logic? A damage suit could ruin her. Probably *would* ruin her.

She climbed out, waiting for him, then realising he couldn't reach the door past his injured arm, she rushed to open it. 'I'm sorry, can I—'

'No, you can't,' he said briskly, unfolding slowly, as she hovered. He walked stiffly around to the front of the car, studied her licence plate, then glanced at her, eyebrows raised. As he turned and limped towards the hospital, Jade stared after him, seething. His message had been clear enough: she could stay or she could run for it, he would find her in the end. She trailed after him slowly, her face grim.

The emergency room was having a busy day of it. Oblivious to his young mother's soothing, a red-faced child howled in one corner, while across the room, a drunk with a bloody nose talked earnestly to the wall. At the desk, a young nurse rolled her eyes at the fair man's bare chest, then handed him a form and a pencil with downcast eyes.

He grinned and took it helplessly. 'But you won't be able to read it—'

'Then I'll do it.' Beside him, Jade held out her hand.

His light grey eyes inspected her face curiously, as he gave her the form. 'Fair enough. Let's find someplace quiet, if we can.' Leading the way around the corner to two straight-backed chairs, he sat carefully. 'Okay, shoot.'

Jade scanned the form. 'Last name?'

'Wykoff—W-y-k-o-f-f.'

'Middle initial?'

'H as in Hubert.'

'Is that what it is?' She stared up at him, horrified.

'Good heavens, no!' He grinned at her, leaned back and shut his eyes.

Jade laughed in spite of herself and looked down again. 'First name?'

'Alexander. Try Zan when you want me.' The hard face tightened, then relaxed again.

Jade bit her lip in sympathy. 'Address?'

The blond brows jerked slightly. 'Let's see, what the devil—oh, Brenton Heights, Apartment Five, Newport. I don't know the zip code yet.'

As she pencilled in the address, Jade raised her eyebrows. That was one of those new condominiums, the ones with the superb views of Newport harbour. So he was a rich jock, then. Did that make things better or worse? 'Age?'

'Thirty-four.'

Her lashes swept up as she turned to inspect him. She might have guessed thirty, but then faint crinkles—his laugh or squint lines, whichever they might be—etched the tan skin at the corners of the wide-set eyes. Add some grey to the straight, thick hair and you'd see him at fifty, she realised. An arresting, ageless face.

'Health insurance?'

The long lips lifted slightly. 'None, sweetheart.' His low voice was serene.

Jade stared at him in dismay, and took a deep breath. 'Okay.'

They finished the form and she brought it back to the desk. The young nurse read over it, frowning. 'Just how will this be paid, miss?'

Jade squared her shoulders. 'I'll be paying for it. Do you want to bill me, or shall I pay it here?'

Jade shifted her weight on the unforgiving seat, and glanced at the clock again. They'd had him in there so long. How bad could it be?

She heard a door click open down the hallway and then his low, enthusiastic voice. 'You mean to say you can tell if it's accident or suicide?'

'Right. In high-speed car wrecks, if he had his foot to the floor, it'll show. The imprint of the shoe will be on the gas pedal, not the brake. The inference is obvious.'

'That's wonderful!' They strolled into view, a small chubby man in a white coat dwarfed by Zan Wykoff, his bare chest now covered by the white sling supporting a large arm cast. 'And you don't mind my calling, if I had any trouble with this strangling, Peter?' He turned to face him as Jade stepped forward, her eyes puzzled.

'Not at all. It'd be my pleasure, Zan. But take it easy for a day or two, will you?' The doctor turned to glance at Jade, his small, clever eyes sweeping across her swiftly, and he smiled broadly. 'But I guess that's your department, isn't it, miss? See if you can get him to eat something when you get him home, and then just put him to bed for the day. He'll be fine tomorrow.'

Jade opened her mouth helplessly, shut it again, as Zan Wykoff spoke. 'Don't worry, Peter,' he said smoothly, his eyes dancing. 'I'll get the best of care. She has a feather touch.'

The doctor grinned. 'Some guys have all the luck! Well, I'll talk to you later, Zan.' He dropped a folder at the desk and hurried off.

'Jerk,' Jade said bitterly.

Zan Wykoff chortled. 'Just getting some of my own back, sweetheart. It may take a while to even the score.'

Jade nodded wearily. 'Okay, Zan. Do you think you can get into the car by yourself? I'll be there in a minute.'

'Where are you going?' The cool grey eyes studied her as he took the keys.

'I'm settling your bill.' She met his gaze steadily.

He nodded slowly. 'Okay.'

It was going to be a hot one for June, Jade noticed, as she trudged back to the car. With the door open, Zan Wykoff slouched in his seat, his feet on the pavement. His lips twitched as he saw her face, but the golden brows were knotted in a shaggy line of pain. They didn't speak until she turned out of the parking lot. 'Brenton Heights?' she asked grimly.

'Please. How much did it cost?' The pale eyes roamed across her profile. Jade concentrated on the road before her and tried not to bite her lip. 'Seven hundred. Broken wrists don't come cheap.'

He breathed heavily. 'Indeed they don't. And this is the least of it.'

She bit her lip, guessing what would come next. How much could he—would he—sue her for, and how much could he take? There was damned little for the taking, besides the house she'd just bought. The airline ticket to

Greece, once she'd cashed it in, would just cover her cheque to the hospital, and that was about it. Once school started in September again, she supposed he could garnish her pay-cheque. And she could—would— sell the bug and offer him the money. She sighed. Thank heavens she hadn't married Fred already! He wouldn't have thanked her, being embroiled in a mess like this. Of course, on the other hand, if they'd been married, he would have never let her drive without insurance.

She sighed again. Somehow she was going to have to placate Zan Wykoff. Settle the score, as he'd put it, without bringing in the lawyers. Make him see that there was only so much blood to be squeezed from a stone. Would he be reasonable? She flicked a glance at him, only to find those cool eyes still on her face.

'It would be nice to have a name for you,' he commented.

'Oh, I'm sorry. Jade—Jade Kinnane.'

'The darling Jade!' he laughed softly.

'I beg your pardon?' She frowned, shifted a gear, and found to her relief that her hand had clearance by his leg this time.

'It's a quote from a grand old sailor, about a racing yacht he loved—a J boat. I can't quite bring it out whole, right now, but it's wonderful. I'll look it up for you some time.' He shifted restlessly and turned to study her. 'But your mother wasn't thinking about that kind of jade when she named you. Was it for your eyes?'

Jade shrugged. 'I suppose so. I understand she'd taken up Oriental flower arranging that year. My father wanted just plain Jane. Mother's tastes were more . . . adventuresome.' She smiled grimly. Some things never change.

'Jade. Jade Kinnane,' he murmured. 'Very nice. Very appropriate . . . Hey, shouldn't you turn there?'

'No,' Jade shook her head. 'All the tourists clog Bellevue this time of day, to see the mansions. This way is longer but quicker. You're new to town, aren't you?'

Leaf shadows and sunlight patterned the narrow road as they spun along between high granite walls. It was nearly one, Jade estimated. If all had gone as planned, she would have completed two or three watercolours by now, and would have been on her way home. If all had gone as planned . . .

'Brand new,' he agreed. 'I arrived late last night, as a matter of fact. I was restless, ended up working instead of sleeping, and decided to wind down with an early morning run. Had a lovely jog, got lost, and was passing a side road when—bam!—my whole life changed,' he smiled wryly.

Jade sighed, nodding, and turned the bug into a long, shaded road with a forbidding 'Private Lane. No Trespassing' notice at the entrance. The road sloped down the grassy hill before them. Through the trees, patches of blue sparkled and shimmered. They rounded a bend, and the harbour opened below them, wide and dazzling, alive with dancing boats. Jade slowed the car, her eyes wide.

They looked down on her favourite part of the harbour, Brenton Cove—the quiet side across from the town. With its deep, still waters bounded by low, jagged cliffs, it reminded her of a small fiord, remote and peaceful.

Across the cove loomed the high, grass-grown walls of Fort Adams, its cannon ports commanding the harbour and the mouth of Narragansett Bay. And beyond the fort, the Newport Bridge traced a springing arc across the sky, its airy grace counterpointing the stubborn weight of the fortress walls. It was a view to steal your breath away, to lift your heart.

She tore her eyes away to inspect the building at the water's edge. The architect had displayed a becoming modesty before this panorama. Choosing to harmonise rather than compete, he had echoed the colours and

thrusts of the broken granite cliffs on which the condominium stood with angular, simple planes of glass and
grey shingles. The resulting design was not an intrusion
on the scenery, but an extrusion of the native rock. Jade
sighed in approval.

'You can stop over there, Jade. Mine's the corner
unit.'

Jade parked, and gathering her courage, walked
around to release him, watched him unfold.

'Come on in.' His voice was quiet, his eyes amused.

She braced herself, shook her head. 'No, thanks, Zan.
You ought to rest, and I've got to get going.'

But Zan's head lifted slightly, and his eyes were no
longer friendly. 'That wasn't an invitation, Jade, that
was an order. I'm not done with you yet. Let's go.' He
jerked his chin towards the door.

She shook her head again, suddenly frightened. What
did she know about this man, after all? 'I'll call you later
if you like, but—'

He leaned into the car and then turned to face her, her
keys dangling from his large fingers. Only his lips smiled.
'If you think you can crash into my life and then speed
away, just like that, you've got another think coming,
Jade. It's not that simple. I'll be inside, when you want to
talk.' He turned away, his golden hair gleaming in the
sunlight, unlocked the door, and disappeared, leaving it
open behind him.

CHAPTER TWO

JADE glared after him, her hands clenched. Damn him! Of all the high-handed—but then she had handled that badly, hadn't she? She had so desperately wanted time to think, time to come up with a plan to placate him. Instead, she'd only aggravated him. She shook her head wretchedly and walked to the door.

Stepping in from the sunlight, she hesitated, blinking in the cool dimness. She had a quick impression of space, and the elegant play of polished woods against rough, pale fabrics in the modern furniture, the rich tones of an Oriental rug. But this was not the time to stop and admire. The long, open room stretched away from her towards glass and sunlight on the waterside, and she could see Zan's wide shoulders and hard profile black against the sky beyond sliding glass doors. Slouching at a table, he turned to stare at her, his face dark against the backlighting.

'Shut the door,' he called. Tilting his head back, he drank from a can, then watched her as she slowly approached across the polished oak floors. 'Want a beer?'

'No, thanks.' She stared down at his cold face. 'Should you be drinking on top of pain pills?'

Zan smiled wryly. 'Kind of you to care, Jade, but I think I can handle one. Consider it part of the medication. Sit down.' He pointed the can at a chair across from him.

She sat, stole a wistful glance at the view beyond the glass, then turned to face him across the table.

'Suppose we start with the basics, Jade,' he said briskly, pushing a large notepad and pen across to her.

'Write down your insurance company, and its address, if you know it.'

Jade bit her lip. 'Why do you want to know?' she hedged desperately.

Zan snorted. 'I think that's obvious, isn't it? I'm willing to chalk the pain and suffering up to experience, and an interesting experience it has been, sweet.' He tipped the can again, his odd, light eyes holding her as he drank. 'But you've disabled me, and at a damned awkward time, too, girl. I'm going to have to sue your company for damages if I don't want to lose my shirt.' His voice hardened. 'Now quit stalling and write it down.'

'I—I haven't got any!' she blurted miserably, her eyes wide and suddenly swimming.

'Ho . . .' Zan breathed softly. He rubbed the cold can slowly across his lips, his eyes ice-grey and narrowed upon her.

Braced for the explosion, Jade endured his gaze, her lips trembling.

'I see,' he said evenly, at last. 'So that's it. That's illegal, isn't it, surely?'

'No.' Her voice sounded tiny in her own ears. 'Not in Rhode Island . . . and I've never had an accident before . . .'

His laugh hissed between his teeth. 'Well, you sure started in a big way, sweet! It may not be illegal, but it sure was stupid. He eyed her grimly. 'So, now I get to gouge my damages out of *you*, not some fat insurance laddies.' He smacked the empty can on the table and stood up abruptly. 'Sure you won't have a beer? This calls for another round.'

'No, I—okay, please,' she changed her mind. At least it would give her a place to put her nervous hands. She watched as he brought them back to the table, one in hand, one tucked in the sling of his cast.

Wedging a can between his hard thighs, Zan flipped

the pop top with his left hand and handed it to her, smiling wryly. 'It opens whole new vistas of experience, doesn't it?'

Jade took it gingerly, her fingers oddly aware of the heat of his legs now fading from the cold metal. She took a polite sip, found she was thirsty, and swallowed a long one. The cold beer fizzed in her empty stomach, seemed to spread out along the veins from her centre like ripples from a dropped stone.

She shivered, then looked up to find his ice-grey gaze waiting for her across the table.

'All right,' he said quietly, his eyes holding her. 'Take the pad, Jade, and write a description of the accident— the location, the time, the date, the speed that you were going, the fact that you jumped the stop sign, and what occurred next.' His hard face was still as a hunting cat when it sees the bird. 'And then sign it.'

Jade licked her lips, thinking rapidly. Without that statement Zan had no case. There had been no witnesses to the accident, and it was his word against hers as to what had happened. She lifted the can and drank, conscious of his eyes on her face. It would be a rotten move on her part, the most selfish thing she'd ever done—but then this was survival. Zan could obviously sustain the damages better than she could, from the looks of this place. And she would still make whatever amends she could afford . . . but that statement would be a mortgage on her life. Once he had that, Zan could strip her of everything. She must not sign. She finished her beer, set it down nervously.

He tossed his off, then crumpled the can absently, his eyes on her face. Jade swallowed, found she couldn't look away as the long fingers crunched and kneaded the aluminium. Zan set the wad of metal delicately between them. 'Well, Jade?'

Resting her hands on the table, she started to rise. 'No, Zan—'

But he moved faster than she expected. A hand like a beartrap shot out to envelop her wrist as he leaned above her, his eyes stony cold. She could feel his breath warm on her face, could feel her eyelids straining to open even wider.

The warm hand squeezed gently, exerted a delicate downward pressure, and she found herself sitting again, knees shaking.

'I don't believe I heard you, the last time,' he drawled softly above her, 'but before you repeat yourself, will you keep in mind three things, Jade? Just remember that it's been a long, hard day for me, that my temper's a little tenuous at the best of times, and . . . that no one knows you're here.' His hand shifted slightly, and his fingers lifted to caress the soft skin along the inside of her wrist.

Jade forced her chin up and felt it quiver. 'You're just trying to scare me,' she said breathlessly.

'Mmm,' he agreed, smiling slightly, his warm fingers stroking her. 'Scandalous how easy it is, too. Your pulse is about a hundred and thirty to the minute, I'd say, right now.'

She hissed, jerked her hand futilely, and his head tilted. 'What's this?' He turned her hand gently, as if inspecting a strange butterfly, stared at the small diamond ring on her finger, then met her eyes again. His eyes were darker now, the pupils wide and black. 'Well, well,' he mocked brightly. 'Engaged, are we? Who's the lucky fellow?'

'You wouldn't know him,' she spat, glaring up at him. 'He doesn't run with your sort!'

Zan threw back his head and laughed. 'My sort,' he murmured. 'That's got a nice desperado ring to it! I like that.' His eyes narrowed again. 'All right, Jade. If you plan to go home to lover boy tonight, start writing.' He tossed her hand aside and moved easily around the table towards her.

She faced forward, refusing to watch his deliberate

advance, her hands clenched on the table to hide their shaking. 'And if I don't?' she asked coolly—but the effect was spoiled as her voice trembled.

Warm fingers closed on the nape of her neck, slid gently up its slender length, rasped in her hair and then travelled slowly down again. A shudder rippled down her spine, and she fought a sudden treacherous urge to lean back against the caress. Damn him!

'If you don't?' his low voice murmured as the warm fingers tightened a touch. 'I'm very tired, Jade. I suppose we'll just sleep on it, and start again in the morning.'

'We?' she choked.

'We,' he agreed caressingly. 'I'm going to get my compensation one way, if not another, sweetheart.'

Jade shut her eyes and laughed breathlessly. 'I'm tired of this gangster talk, Zan. Shut up, will you?'

'Then just go ahead and write it, sweet.' His fingers wandered up her neck again. 'All I want is the truth, you know.'

She shuddered. 'Don't *do* that!'

'Do what I ask, or I'll do what I please, Jade.' The low voice had dropped; it had a velvety, oddly menacing tone to it now. The warm fingers slid inside her shirt, traced the collarbone slowly out to her shoulder point.

She tried to stand, but the fingers pressed down gently, pinning her to the chair. She drew a shaky breath. 'I'll scream!'

He laughed huskily. 'Scream away, sweetheart. There's no one home next door. They're gone for the week.' The ruthless fingers found her hairclip, fumbled gently, stopped to press her down again, found the catch and sprang it. Her heavy hair slid down across her shoulders in silken waves, and she could hear his breath quicken behind and above her now, as she blinked back the tears. This was mad, it wasn't happening, it was all a cruel joke! The sane and sunny world beyond the glass was the real world; this dim room, the hypnotic, dominating fingers were some nightmare—she'd wake any second now. Jade shook her head dizzily as the fingers combed through her hair, held it out to the light and dropped it.

She swallowed and squared her shoulders. 'Zan, stop it! I'm warning you, stop it,' she faltered. 'I'm going to start kicking and clawing in a minute, and I'm going straight for your damaged arm. Don't make me hurt you!'

His breath hissed and then the weight on her shoulders increased as he leaned against her, shaking with silent laughter. Jade swallowed a scream of pure frustration—*damn him!*—and then flinched as a heavy arm slid around her chest, pinning her arms to her sides, flattening her breasts against his golden forearm. Her nipples lifted and hardened beneath her thin shirt as a wave of hot terror swept through her.

'Think I can't lick you with one arm behind my back, Jade?' he purred in her ear. 'I think I'll lick you all over! Forget the paper.' She jerked as his warm tongue and then his lips scorched her shoulder, traced a languid, burning line up the side of her throat.

'All *right*! *Please!* All right, Zan!' she panted, twisting her head away. 'I'll do it—stop!' She blinked desperately as the tears overflowed. Oh, *damn* him!

The warm lips paused, brushed her jawline slowly and then lifted away. 'I was afraid you'd say that,' he sighed politely. The imprisoning arm eased a little.

Jade took a deep, shuddering breath. 'What do you want me to write?' she muttered.

The arm lifted away. Fingers rested lightly on her shoulder again, tapped a nervous dance. 'Mmm . . . all right.' Above her, he took a deep, deliberate breath. 'On the morning of June 8, I, Jade Kinnane . . .'

But the tear-blurred handwriting was too shaky to be her own. Jade's pen reached the 'I', wobbled, then scrawled *'hate you!'* in two-inch letters, and underlined it savagely. She dropped the pen and shut her eyes as the fingers closed gently on her shoulder again.

'Yes, I know,' Zan murmured patiently. Leaning past her to rip the sheet off the pad, he cocked his head down to examine her tear-stained face with cool grey eyes. The hard lips twitched and his face lifted out of sight again. Fingers brushed the top of her head with a nervous, almost gentle touch and fell away. 'Try it again, Jade,' the voice soothed. 'We've got hours left and lots of paper . . . On the morning of . . .'

Zan leaned above her, his cast grazing the top of her head as he read the statement. Jade shut her eyes, but felt him nod. 'That's very good, sweet,' he murmured. 'Did we get anything wrong, leave anything out?' She shook her head wearily. 'Good. Then sign it, Jade, and you can go home.'

She stared at the pen, stared at the free blue world beyond the glass as his hand found her shoulder again, kneading encouragement. Shuddering, she lifted the pen and signed. Zan reached out to take the pad, carried it beyond her reach, and returned to sit heavily beside her. In the dim light, his hard face had a greenish cast beneath the tan. He leaned his head on his hand and studied her face. 'Whew!' His long gold lashes swept down to cover the ice-grey eyes. 'Do you type, by the way, sweet?' he murmured dreamily.

Her chair smashed over with a bang as Jade leaped to her feet. 'You are—you—I hate you!' she stuttered, whirling away from him. He didn't move.

But the cool voice stopped her as she reached the door. 'Jade, do you want your car keys?'

Teeth showing in a white snarl, she jerked to face him. 'Yes!'

His face was in darkness, but the late sunlight beyond gleamed through his tousled hair, edging his head with rough silver. 'They're on the bookcase to the left of the door,' he called quietly. 'Come see me about ten tomorrow, and I'll tell you what I want.' The dark face turned back to the water. She was dismissed.

CHAPTER THREE

JADE swung her head down, brushed her hair out, righted herself and brushed some more until it crackled in electric waves across her shoulders. She shook it back—there'd be time enough to braid it after breakfast—and surveyed herself in the mirror. The faint shadows beneath her jade-green eyes made them look larger. Across her short nose, the sprinkling of freckles stood out as if she were paler today. She wrinkled her nose. She hadn't slept well these last two nights—not since the day of the accident.

After that terrifying interview, she had tottered numbly home to sleep the clock around, and had woken from a night of bad dreams certain of one fact, and one fact alone: she would not report to Zan Wykoff at ten o'clock as he'd commanded—she would never go near him in her whole life again, if she had any say in the matter! The man was obviously dangerous, if not an outright lunatic.

And what he planned to do with her confession was anybody's guess. She was not sticking around to find out. She was going to Greece, if she had to swim to get there. With an ocean between them, and with Fred's sane and soothing advice, she would sort out the legal ramifications of her wretched accident, and the confession that Zan now held. The first thing to do was escape.

And that required money. Yesterday had been a mad scramble to raise enough cash to cover Zan's hospital bill and her flight as well.

Jade had not even considered asking her parents for help. Her father was drained, financially as well as emotionally, from the bitter divorce of this spring. And

she was not on speaking terms with her mother yet. That
left only her car and her best seascapes, the ones she'd
never meant to sell, as sources of revenue. So she had
sold her VW to a local car dealer for a sum just this side
of insult, and had stripped her apartment walls of the
framed watercolours, carting them down the hill to the
gallery near the waterfront. With any luck at all, they
would sell this weekend when the tourists flocked into
town.

In the meantime, she had had to cash in her airline
ticket to cover the cheque she had given the hospital.
That had been a nasty moment . . . But her reservation
was still good, would be good until the afternoon before
the flight. All she needed was money.

And luck . . . Jade stared grimly at her pale face in the
mirror. The strain of yesterday's financial dealings had
been compounded by her dread of running into Zan
Wykoff on the street. Newport was a small town really.
With all of its action centring around the waterfront, one
bumped continually into the same people. And there
was one person she'd bumped once too often already
. . . Turning to her closet, Jade chose a white Indian
cotton blouse to go with her khaki shorts. Well, with any
luck at all, she would be in Greece by the time Zan
tracked down her address through her licence plates.
Thank God her phone number was unlisted! But it
would be close, no doubt about it. She would just have to
lie low and pray that Zan had forgotten those numbers.
Padding into the kitchen, Jade frowned. She had the
awful conviction that he hadn't . . .

She jumped at the rap on the door. It was quick,
officious. 'Telegram.' It was a boy's voice, light and
bored.

Jade breathed thankfully, then felt her relief turn to
worry—a telegram? Fred. It must be from Fred, her
father always phoned. 'Just a minute,' she called, sliding
the bolt. The door swung back to reveal a white sling,

a laughing face—'*Oh!*' She slammed it viciously as a heavy shoe jammed down in the opening. The door rebounded, slammed open as she retreated across the room.

Zan was laughing too hard to move; he leaned against the doorframe, enormous in her small kitchen, and howled, gasping for air, his grey eyes squeezed tight. '—sucker,' he gasped finally. 'How have you lived this long?'

'Get out!' Back to the sink, Jade glared at him, eyes wild. 'Get out, or I'll scream!' she stormed, stamping her foot hysterically. 'I mean it, Zan! Get out!'

Her words set him off again, and he yelped until the wall shook, shambled forward to collapse in a chair with a groan, and gulped air, his eyes crinkling as he stared at her. 'I never . . . thought I could pull it off!' he panted blissfully.

So the lines at his eyes were laughter lines, Jade concluded, taking a deep breath. *I hate him!* she thought viciously. Her heart's stampede was slowing to a brisk canter, and she took her eyes off him to flick a glance at the phone across the kitchen. Could she make it?

His golden head swung to follow her gaze, turned back to inspect her. The ice-grey eyes were still dancing. He shook his head. 'No, you couldn't make it,' he told her gently. 'And you don't want the cops anyway.'

'Don't be so sure!' she snarled at him.

But fumbling at his pocket, Zan pulled out a folded paper and tossed it on the table. 'The time for the cops was two days ago, Jade, and I'm the sucker who should have called them. I expect they'll be a bit vexed at my tardiness, but they'll still be interested in your confession.' He shoved the paper towards her a few inches, his face polite. 'That's your copy. I've got several more.'

Jade licked her lips and shook her hair back from her face. 'You bastard,' she commented. 'What do you want?'

His long lips twitched at her words, and she flinched as the laser beam eyes focussed on her bare feet, climbing her long legs like a warm, slow spotlight. The deliberate gaze was more caress than inspection, and her pulse accelerated even as her temper flared. As his eyes stroked her breasts, she could feel the hot blood rise to sweep up her throat and flame in her cheeks. She raised her head proudly, her eyes blazing back at him as she braced herself for the insult.

Zan held her flashing eyes for a long moment, his face thoughtful. 'I've always wanted to blackmail a beautiful girl,' he remarked softly. 'What about breakfast?' The grey eyes danced. 'Have you ever tried to crack an egg with one hand—the left one?'

Jade's breath hissed out slowly. Unclenching her hands, she reached for the eggs. 'I can think of about two thousand men I'd have rather run over than you, Zan Wykoff,' she murmured bitterly. 'Maybe three thousand!'

Zan leaned back to heave a sigh. 'That was superb. I'm a new man, Jade.'

'That would have to be an improvement,' she growled, pouring the coffee. She set a cup before him, then sat down across from him to drink her own, her eyes wary. So what was coming next?

The light eyes inspected her idly as he sipped, then moved to roam slowly over the kitchen and beyond into her small living room, with its white walls and hanging plants. The thick golden brows twitched gently as some conclusion was reached, then the eyes returned to her face.

She scowled impatiently. 'How did you find me, Zan?' she demanded finally.

He smiled gently and held out his cup. 'Is there any more of this, Jade? It's very good.'

He sugared his second cup clumsily, his eyes thoughtful. Finally his lips curled. 'I had so many ways to find you, Jade, it took me a day to make up my mind which one I'd use.'

'Such as?' she challenged.

'Well, if I'd been in a mood to bar-hop, I'd have wandered into three or four of the swanker bars on the waterfront, and asked the bartenders if they know a long, lean redhead, with eyes like emerald daggers.' He grinned evilly. 'I've never known a bartender who could tell red hair from auburn.'

She scowled. 'And if it turned out that I'm the type who drinks alone?'

'Oh, I suppose next I'd have found the nearest art store, asked them if they knew where I could find you. How many people of your description do you think buy artist-grade Winsor & Newton watercolours, in a town this size?'

Jade bit her lip. That approach would have hit paydirt. Wanda, her friend who worked there, was a fool for big fair men. She would have fingered Jade immediately.

Oblivious to its ominous creakings, Zan leaned back in his chair to inspect the ceiling. 'Or I could have called the private school whose decal is on the back window of your bug, and asked them about you.' He let the chair down to examine her stony face with interest. 'You know, for a woman who lunges around, blithely assaulting men with a deadly weapon—and that's exactly what a car is, Jade—you show a real deficiency of criminal skills,' he said reproachfully.

Jade gathered up the coffee cups and slammed them into the sink. 'But you didn't use any of those methods, did you?' she said viciously.

'No . . .' he drawled, 'actually I got a street map and looked up the address that's printed on this cheque.' He pulled a familiar-coloured cheque from his pocket and tossed it on the table.

'*Where* did you get this?' Jade snatched it up incredulously. It was hers all right, made out to the local grocery store and dated nearly a month ago.

'It's not a good practice to leave your latest bank statement in the pocket of your car, Jade. Not if you allow strangers to sit there unattended.'

'You *snoop*!' she gasped, crushing the cheque into a small wad.

Zan nodded. His face was slowly changing, the mischief of the last few minutes freezing into something harder. 'It's one way to learn many useful facts.' The steely eyes drilled into her. 'One fact I learned about you, Jade, is that, four days ago, you had only nine dollars in that account. And so now there is one thing I have to know,' he murmured gently, '—will that cheque you gave them bounce?'

'No!' she snapped, spinning away from him.

'Where did you get the money to cover it—lover boy?' he jeered softly.

'*No*, damn you! And it's none of your business.' Jade stalked from the kitchen, and through to her bedroom, where she began to braid her hair back with ruthless hands.

Zan leaned in the doorway behind her, rubbing his right hand where it peeped from the cast. 'Did you sell your watercolours?' he asked idly.

She glared at him desperately in the mirror. He was getting too close to her escape plans by far. '*What* watercolours?'

'The ones that hung on the walls here. I've counted six empty nails, so far.'

Didn't he miss anything? 'That's—none . . . of . . . your . . . *business*,' she grated. 'I've paid the bill—that's all you need to know.'

Behind her, his light eyes were roving the room. She saw them stop, then narrow, as they found Fred's photograph on the wall by her bed. 'So that's lover boy,' he remarked mildly. 'I lost sleep for nothing.'

'And what do you mean by *that*?' she gasped.

'After you left the other day, every time I heard a sound, I woke up—kept thinking it was lover boy pounding on my door, wanting to come pound my head in.' The grey eyes measured her. 'And then all yesterday I stayed home, figuring he'd want to see me.'

'Sounds like you had a guilty conscience.' Jade found she could not look away, the strange eyes in the mirror held her.

His lips twitched in a faint, crooked smile. 'I guess I did. If you'd been mine, and someone bullied you that way, *I'd* have wanted to do some pounding.' The ice eyes narrowed. 'But I take it lover boy's too civilised for that kind of reaction? Is that how your tastes run—to civilised boys?'

He flinched as the hairbrush smashed off the wall beside him. 'You are—such an *unspeakable* jerk that there aren't *words* to describe you!' Jade raved, starting for him, her hands clenched. 'I am *sick* of this harassment! What do you *want*?' Tears of rage gleamed in her eyes as she stopped before him, her head thrown back.

His eyes were unreadable, as he stared down at her. The thick brows clenched and relaxed again, and his gaze dropped to her small feet. 'I guess, Jade, the first thing I want . . . is your pardon,' he murmured slowly, the pale eyes lifting to hers again. 'I'm out of line, as usual. It's a bad habit.' He turned away and stepped into her living room, leaned on the window sill to inspect the street below. 'The second thing I want is your help,' he remarked gently.

Jade crossed her arms and leaned in the doorway, shaking her head. 'I don't believe you, Zan Wykoff,' she breathed, staring at him. 'You break in here to threaten me, insult me, terrorise me, and then you have the nerve to say you want my help! Just what kind of a nut are you?'

He turned to face her, flinched as his head brushed a

hanging fern, then stood still, the tender green caressing one cheek as the sun gilded the other. His strange eyes were wide and wary on her face, and Jade's head lifted in sudden appreciation. He looked like a startled faun, or a young lion in his prime, shining with a wild and ruthless innocence. *I've got to paint that!* she thought urgently. It was a long time since she'd done a portrait, but this one she must do.

'What's the matter?' Zan asked huskily. The thick eyebrows lifted, as his voice broke the spell.

Jade looked away, moved aimlessly, then turned to consult her favourite watercolour. She stared at the bare nail blankly and bit her lip. *Damn* him. 'What do you want of me, Zan?' she asked helplessly, turning to face him again. 'I've done the damage, and I'm sorry, but what can I do? I can't heal bones. And I haven't got a penny to give you.'

He sat down slowly on her sofa, his cool eyes holding her gaze. 'You've got time, haven't you?' he asked softly. 'You ran me down on a Wednesday. At that hour, you were either going home from a lover or going to paint—the latter, I suspect, with your kit in the car. You spent half the day with me and never once looked at your watch. And now here it's a Friday, nine in the morning, and again you're not off working. And you were here last night, when I walked by your window. So I'd guess you're a teacher or a student on holiday, Jade.' The laser eyes roved across her face. 'But you're just a year or two too old to be a college girl, and you don't giggle. You've got an air of command—you can send a man off to wait in the car and expect to be obeyed, and you're surprised each time I don't follow orders. That tells me something about lover boy, and something about you. I'd say you're a teacher, with your summer off, and I want it. It's as simple as that.'

Jade pulled a shaky breath, tried to jog her numbed brains, and swallowed. She couldn't tear her eyes away from Zan's hypnotic gaze. She had the awful conviction that, if he wanted to, he could strip her with those cold eyes, slice down past cloth, and convention and flesh to the bone, lay her soul out to quiver and flop like a fish tossed gasping on the beach. She shut her eyes. 'Just tell me what you're getting at, Zan. Please!'

'I'm a writer, Jade.' His long lips twitched as her eyes flashed open to gape at him. 'And now I can't write.' His left hand stole across to feel the trapped fingers. He smiled ruefully. 'I need a secretary, someone to type for me.'

Jade fought a sudden urge to laugh. Or maybe it was hysteria. All this melodrama had been leading up to *this*? 'But, Zan, why didn't you just say so? Look, I'll rent you a dictaphone—I can raise the money somehow. And I'll find someone who can type it out for you . . .'

But he was shaking his head angrily. 'I can't work that way, Jade—dictating. I have to see the words before me as I write. I stop and re-read it a dozen times as I go along, change a word here, a phrase there. I have to refer back to the plot to keep in mind where I'm going— it can't be locked away in a black box where I can't see it, till a typist gets around to it three days later.' He clenched his teeth and glared at her. 'I can't even drive my damned car to get the work *to* a blasted typist!' He jerked to his feet and paced to the window. 'I need someone who will sit and type, while I read it over her shoulder—someone to delete, and correct, and cut and tape as I direct. I need a pair of hands. I need you.' The laser eyes shot out to warm her face.

Jade shook her head slowly. 'But I'm not going to be here, Zan. I'm off to marry Fred in Greece next week.'

Zan's golden head lifted dangerously. The laser beam was narrowing, focussing to burn a path through her eyes and into her mind. 'Well, isn't that just too bad?' he drawled softly. 'Because I do believe you'll have to change your plans, Jade. Just as you've changed mine.'

Jade shook her head desperately. 'Zan, look, I'll get a loan, then . . . somehow, hire you a secretary . . .'

He laughed, paced towards her restlessly, didn't seem to notice as she edged away from him along the wall. He leaned in the kitchen doorway and inspected the door-frame. 'Just how much do you think a live-in secretary costs nowadays, girl?' he asked idly. 'Whatever it is, you obviously haven't got it.'

'Live-in? What do you mean?'

The cool eyes studied her. 'I write in the mornings, Jade. If it goes well, I write all day. If it doesn't, I go play, and it usually comes to me that night. You expect me to call up some secretary at three a.m. and tell her to trot right over? Secretaries are a flighty bunch, girl. They're off at the disco, or out on a date, or otherwise unavail-able. I want someone I can depend on and use, day or night. I want you.'

'No!' Jade gritted her teeth and shook her head again. 'No, Zan, you can't make me do this!'

But turning to face her, Zan seemed to expand to fill the doorway as he slowly straightened and lifted his head. And now she realised why he was there. It was the only way out. 'Oh, yes I can make you, Jade,' he said softly. His low voice was falling, dropping to that husky tone she dreaded, and suddenly she could feel her heart thumping in her breast.

Zan smiled gently. 'I can do it civilised, by hiring a lawyer and stripping you of every penny you've ever made or hope to make, Jade. And if you marry lover boy, I'll see if I can tap his bank account, too.' The cold eyes roved her white face. 'Anyone who marries you should expect to pay, after all. Through the wallet, if not otherwise.' His voice was a caressing burr now, almost a whisper. 'That's the civilised method to make you do what I want, Jade. The other way is with my bare hands. That's the method I favour.'

Jade put a hand on the wall to steady herself, and shut

her eyes to shut him out. Her brain was whirling. 'He's got you,' a small voice inside her chanted. 'He's got you.' And it was not a lawsuit that she feared now.

Her eyes flashed open as she heard him move, but Zan was just making himself comfortable. He slouched back against the doorframe, obviously prepared to wait all day. His brows bunched. 'Well, Jade?'

She took a deep breath. She'd felt like this as a child on the high diving-board, staring down at the distant blue water. Once you were up there, there was no backing down. You had to jump. She took another breath. Well, so be it . . . 'Zan.'

'Mm?'

'If—and I mean if—I do this, there are two things you'll have to promise . . .'

The ice eyes widened in question. 'Yes?'

'First, that you don't expect me to—to live there with you. We're only about a mile and a half apart, and I could come when you call, day or night.' Crossing her arms, she hugged herself, trying not to shiver. 'Second, is that you don't ever touch me again. I don't care to be manhandled.'

Zan was silent as she waited tensely. Finally he spoke. 'I don't believe you're in a position to extract promises, Jade.'

'I *won't* live there. I won't!'

His lips twitched as he studied her flushed face. 'But you'll drop whatever you're doing, and come when I call, day or night?'

She swallowed. 'Yes.'

His look was doubtful, but slowly he nodded. 'We'll try it that way, then.'

'And you won't—'

'Jade.' His cold eyes mocked her. 'There's only one thing I really want—and that's to finish my book by the end of August.'

She looked down at her feet, her face hot.

His low voice was amused. 'You help me to finish it, and we'll call the debt square. That I will promise.'

Looking up, she found he was smiling. 'You'd give me my statement back?'

Something flickered in his eyes, but he nodded.

It was time to take the plunge. Jade took a deep breath. 'All right, then, Zan. When do we start?'

But he was moving already, looming above her. 'When do we start, she says!' A big hand reached out to sweep her into the kitchen before him. 'Right now. Yesterday! Let's *go*, Jade.'

'*Wait* a minute!' She dug in her heels and wheeled to face him, putting up a hand to block the charge. 'May I put on some shoes?' she asked breathlessly.

Zan scowled, grey eyes electric. 'Only if you hurry.' He paced the kitchen while she ran to find them, and then herded her out of the door and down the stairs.

CHAPTER FOUR

'So you write murder mysteries!' Jade looked up from the sheet of paper in Zan's typewriter. His typing stopped in mid-sentence with a long line of exclamation marks and a few vicious-looking nonsense words, but the story above Zan's explosion seemed to concern an unidentified victim despatched by an inexplicable method.

Across the patio, Zan turned his back on the view to face her; 'The preferred label is thriller.'

Jade studied his face. He looked restless, almost irritated. 'What's the difference?'

'Less mystery, more mayhem, no clever old ladies allowed. Now why don't you just get yourself comfortable there and we'll get started . . .' He turned back to the harbour.

Jade sat down reluctantly. It was too lovely out here on the condominium's patio, just a few feet above the water, to think of working. Zan had placed the typewriter on a round picnic table facing the harbour. Even as she looked up, a red catamaran dodged through the boats moored in the cove and wheeled out into the open blue beyond. She sighed. This was going to be a hard way to pass a summer, chained to a typewriter in sight of so much freedom.

'Ready?' Zan's shadow fell across the table as he loomed behind her.

Suppressing a shiver, Jade nodded. She would have to relax. She couldn't flinch every time Zan walked up behind her like that. But she'd half expected warm fingers to close on the nape of her neck for a second there.

Black and motionless, his shadow lay across her. 'He's still warm.'

'What?'

'Dammit it, Jade, start typing!'

'Oh!' She blushed, and reaching for the keys, pecked out the sentence carefully.

Zan's shadow shook its head glumly and then stilled. 'Next paragraph: "That's hardly surprising; look at . . ."' Still dictating, Zan turned away from her and began to pace the patio, his low voice carrying clearly above the lap of the wavelets on the rocks below. Jade's fingers pattered behind him like a short-legged puppy chasing a long-legged master across the pages and the hours.

'What's this town—no, don't *type* this, Jade, I'm talking to you!' Zan scowled as she looked up at him.

'Well, how should I know the difference!' she flared, crossing out the first words of his question.

'Use your ears. What's this town like in December?'

'Why?'

'Because at this rate we'll still be here, tap-tapping our way into the fifth chapter by Christmas!' Shaking dark gold hair off his forehead, Zan leaned back against the low wall that enclosed the patio and scowled down at his large brown feet. He looked up at her stricken face, and laughed suddenly. 'Don't look like that! I'll let you off the patio by October, Jade. We'll order a cord of wood and work by the fireplace. Might be rather cosy.' His grey eyes danced.

Jade found her breath in a rush. 'If I thought I was going to be here with you in December, Zan, I'd hang this typewriter around my neck and jump off the dock right now! Cosy be damned!' She watched his grin widen with blazing eyes. He was just baiting her, of course. She pushed back her chair and stood up. 'Break time,' she announced.

'All right,' he agreed amiably. Pushing off the wall, he

ambled over to the pile of manuscript on the table and began to re-read it, his good hand massaging the back of his neck.

Jade studied his wide shoulders for a moment and then stepped through the open glass doors and into the room beyond. She paused, blinking in the cool and welcome dimness. It was the first chance she had really had to study the room. Zan had rushed her straight through and out to the patio this morning, and the other time . . .

The ground floor of the condo was a clean, open L-shape. She stood in the corner of the L—the dining area—by the table where Zan and she had played out their battle of wills the other day. To her right, an airy, modern kitchen formed the rest of the short leg of the L, the leg that faced the water. One could stand at the counter and chop onions while staring out the large windows which gave on the patio and the cove beyond. A good way to lose a fingertip, come to think of it.

The long leg of the L stretched away from the water towards the entrance on the inland side of the condo. From the dining room, an open, varnished wood stairway climbed the wall, leading up to a second floor. And beyond the stairway, as it approached the front door, dining room merged with and became living room.

This distinction was created by a change in level—the living room was three steps lower than the rest of this floor. Cream-coloured modular sofas outlined this rectangular pit, and above it, the ceiling was cut away. One looked up two storeys to a cedar-beamed roof with a large, gleaming skylight. The inland wall of the pit was stone—a chimney, in fact, rising grey and rugged above the massive fireplace at its base. The stone bank in front of the chimney formed a wall-length bench as well as the hearth.

Jade stepped down into the pit, her feet sinking into

the soft wool of a red and gold Oriental rug. It would be cosy indeed here in winter, with a fire going.

'Go around the fireplace to your right, and you'll find a bathroom, if you want to powder your nose, Jade.' Zan wandered into the kitchen. 'Are you hungry yet?' he called.

'No.'

'That's good, 'cause I've eaten everything in the house. We'll have to go shopping later.'

We? Jade looked up, eyes narrowed, but Zan was out of sight around the corner.

'What about a soda?' he called.

'Please.' She prowled nervously into the entrance way past the chimney, and studied the front door with wistful eyes. What had she got herself into? Her green eyes fell on the bookcase where Zan had left her keys the other day, and a photograph on the top shelf caught her attention. Zan stood on a beach, laughing up at the girl who sat on his shoulders. Hands twined in his hair, she mugged at the camera, her elfin face sparkling with mischief. Jade felt an odd twinge. Had she and Fred ever looked that happy together?

She studied Zan. How old was he there? The girl's heels kicked against a chest as muscular and hairy as the one she had seen two days ago. His face was perhaps a little younger, but maybe it was just his happiness that made it seem so. No more than five years ago, Jade decided, if that. The girl's age was harder to guess— middle twenties, maybe even a little older. She was a delicate blonde who would look fine at fifty. Jade sighed.

'That's Mona, the temptress who got me into this mess.' Zan spoke behind her.

Damn, but he was quiet! Jade took a steadying breath before she turned to face him. Zan was half smiling, half glaring at the photo above Jade's head. He absently handed her a Coke.

'Mess?' she asked.

'We're buying this condo together. I'm beginning to wonder if it's such a bright idea.' He made a wry face at the photo.

'It's a stunning place.'

'Yes,' he agreed dryly. 'With payments to match. Somehow I'm feeling less secure about making my ends meet than I was three days ago.' Putting a big hand on her arm, he eased her past him towards the patio. 'Speaking of which, it's back to the grind, girl.'

Jade bit her bottom lip. 'What happens if you don't finish this book by the end of August, Zan?'

'What do you care?' The ice-grey eyes studied her face with lazy interest.

'I do care,' her eyes dropped to his cast. 'If anyone got you into this mess, it was me.'

'So you'll just have to get me out again.' He shooed her ahead of him. 'Let's get writing.'

She had got him into this mess, so now she would help him out of it. There was a rough justice there that Jade couldn't deny, even if she had been blackmailed into paying her debt. But as the hours passed and her hesitant fingers chased after Zan's story, a suspicion took root and began to grow: could she have been conned?

It was no wonder that Zan could sometimes act like a Mafia hit-man with a toothache. Violence was his subject matter. The question was, did the menacing, velvet-voiced stranger who had wrung the confession out of her, who had come this morning to claim her help and her summer—did he actually exist? Was he the dark side that balanced the glancing, off beat sense of humour, the kindness she sensed in this man who paced before her now, or just a convincing fiction? Was Zan potentially dangerous if provoked, or merely a clever joker? Jade would have given a lot to know which.

'Cripes, but you're slow! Is that the fastest you can type?' Zan stopped by the table to glare down at her.

'I'm falling all over myself, thinking at normal speed and talking in slow motion!'

Jade flexed aching fingers and scowled back at him. She had never typed so fast nor so long in her whole life, and still the brute wasn't satisfied! 'That's as fast as I go,' she pronounced defiantly. 'What you see is what you get.'

She scraped back her chair and bounced to her feet. Zan held his ground as she stood, and she found herself suddenly toe to toe with him, her head thrown back so she could see his mocking face. 'I suggest that the next time you throw yourself in front of a car, Zan, you check the driver's typing skills beforehand if—'

Zan's brows bristled and shot skyward. '*Throw* myself in front of a car . . . ?' he repeated incredulously, his eyes widening and gleaming now with a murderous light as he leaned towards her. 'For a homicidal driver, you've got some gall, Jade!' He leaned even closer; their noses were nearly touching now. His golden brows twitched gently. '—And you've *no* sense of self preservation whatsoever, to go insulting your victim in his own den,' he drawled softly. Cocking his head, he studied her flushed face with cool eyes. 'Apart from your driving, I can certainly tell you're a woman, too.'

'What?' Jade blinked at the subject change.

'Mm-hm.' His hand touched her face. Hooking a gentle finger under her jaw, he traced the bone out towards her pointed chin. 'I mean there are other . . . indications, but right now you're exhibiting one of the most endearing traits of the sex.'

His finger stroked a small circle, teasing the soft skin just under her chin. 'Get a woman angry and she sticks her trusting little chin out. Men learn not to do that by fifth grade.' He grinned maddeningly.

His taunt called forth an ugly memory—an image of a livid, foxy face and the pain that followed. 'Huh!' Jade tossed her head aside, but Zan's fingers closed on her chin, swinging her back to face him. His eyes sharpened as she clenched her jaws to fight the trembling that was vibrating up from her stomach. And why did he frighten her so? He was just a big clown, after all . . . Wasn't he? She jerked her chin again, but oblivious to her attempts to escape, he simply swung her face the other way, his grey eyes intent on her cheeks.

'Now is that anger, or have we succeeded in frying you?' Zan murmured to himself. 'Your skin's almost transparent, Jade. It's lovely to watch the colour ebb and flow. It's surely high tide right now.' He freed her chin. 'Turn around.'

Sighing in exasperation, Jade obeyed. It was simpler than arguing with him, she began to suspect. She flinched as his hand closed on her braid, and flipped it over her shoulder. Light and cool, Zan's fingers brushed the back of her neck, and she shuddered in spite of herself.

'Fried!' he gloated. 'Or nearly so. Will you let me call you Red now?'

'No, you jerk!' She ducked out from under his hand. 'Am I really?'

'Go see for yourself. There's a hand mirror in the bathroom upstairs.' He turned back to the manuscript, and grateful for the excuse to flee, Jade hurried away.

The varnished stairway led up from the dining room to an open hallway above. One side of this passage was a waist-high wall. Leaning over it, she looked down on the living room pit below.

Off the hall on the water side of the floor were two bedrooms, and Jade peeped in through their open doors. The smaller one had the unused look of a guest room—bed tightly made and bureau clear. Blue curtains lined the glass seaward wall, shutting out a balcony and the view beyond.

The white-walled, book-strewn corner bedroom was obviously Zan's. Entranced, Jade paused in the doorway. Sliding glass doors formed the waterside wall.

Beyond the open curtains she could see a narrow balcony that overlooked the patio below and the harbour. What a view! The big modern bed faced that view, with a mountain of pillows piled along the headboard. She pictured Zan propped up in bed at night, staring out at the lighted fairy crown of the Newport Bridge, sea breeze whispering in through the open doors. At least that was how she would lie, if she owned such a room.

Jade turned away. Now where was that bathroom? Circling the gallery, she found it above the bathroom on the first floor, tucked behind the two-storey chimney wall.

In the bathroom's mirrored walls, she inspected herself with loathing. How could she have forgotten a hat? Her cheeks might not peel, but the tip of her nose was a lost cause. She glanced around for the hand mirror and a gleam of silver caught her eye.

She picked up the mirror gingerly. She knew whose this was, even before she saw the delicate engraving along the handle—'Mona.' She stared into the oval glass. Framed by ornate scrolls of sterling silver, a vivid face leaped back at her, its green eyes ironic. 'Yes, I know,' she told the mirror, 'we clash. You want your snow mistress back.' And where *was* the silvery blonde who matched this mirror? She swung around to study the back of her neck. Fried was the word for it! Jade set down the mirror and began to undo her braid. At least she could hide the damage.

'Hey, Red!' Zan's bellow sounded from below.

Jade gritted her teeth. There was no way she'd answer to that name.

There was a moment of silence. 'Green?' he tried doubtfully.

She smiled in spite of herself. 'You're getting warm,' she called back, stepping into the hallway.

'Jade!' His voice held a note of delighted recollection.

'You've got it!' she laughed, then leaning over the balcony, she caught her breath.

Flat on his back, Zan lounged directly below her on the sofa, his good arm tucked behind his head. He smiled up at her lazily. That's how a man's supposed to look, she thought rapidly, taking in those wide shoulders tapering to narrow hips, the long, hard legs fuzzed with pale gold. So why don't more men look like that? Suddenly conscious of the silence, she met his sleepy gaze.

'I like your hair like that, Rapunzel,' he said softly.

'Are you all right?' she asked doubtfully, ignoring the compliment.

He shook his head, grey eyes mournful.

'What's the matter, Zan?' Could his arm be hurting him?

'Advanced starvation,' he pronounced weakly. 'We've got to go shopping—I can't write on an empty stomach.'

Jade stared down at him in exasperation. 'Zan, I signed on as a typist, not a shopping service! That's not part of the deal.'

His eyes narrowed to a beam of cold light, as his lips shaped a hard line. 'Jade, as far as I see it, you are here to help me do any and everything I could do for myself three days ago, before we . . . bumped into each other,' he clipped out. He tapped his cast bitterly. 'You'll have noticed I can't straighten the elbow joint. *You* try shifting a car's stickshift like that!'

Jade nibbled her bottom lip. 'I didn't think of that . . . I'm sorry.' She brushed her hair back from her eyes. 'I'm afraid I've sold my car . . .'

Zan's eyebrows jumped, but he nodded approval. 'Just as well. You wouldn't have gotten *me* in that uninsured death-trap again.'

'*Death*-trap!' she sputtered.

He rolled over and stood up. 'Let's go, Jade,' he

commanded, holding out his arm and his cast. 'Jump—
I'll catch you.'

'Oh, thanks. You'd look terrific in double casts!' she
laughed down at him.

He grinned. 'Then I'd *really* be at your mercy!' His
smile faded. 'Offer withdrawn.' He wandered off towards the kitchen.

'Drive *that*? You've got to be kidding, Zan!' Jade
stared at the teardrop shape of the racy old Porsche. In
the dusk of the garage, the antique sports car gleamed a
deep forest green.

'I am not. You'll drive it and like it, before I'm done
with you, sweet.' Zan stepped into the garage, trailing
his fingers along the car's sleek curves in an absent
caress. 'I bought it just to match your eyes, Jade. You've
got to drive it.' He turned to face her, eyebrows up.
'Now put your hand out and come forward slowly . . .
and whatever you may feel, act confident. She can sense
fear in an instant.' He jerked his chin gently. 'Come
on.'

Jade shook her head and stepped forward, half expecting the Porsche to growl and take a nip at her legs.
She stopped by the left door, eyeing Zan across the low
top.

'By Jove, Jade,' he murmured in a fruity English
accent, his eyes wide, 'I believe she likes you! She
doesn't usually take to strangers.'

She scowled at him. 'Did you remember to tell the
doctor that you landed on your head the other day, Zan?
He must have some kind of pill that will help you.'

His face was solemn. 'There's no cure for what ails
me, sweet.' His lips twitched faintly. 'It's terminal every
time. Get in.'

The inside of the Porsche reminded her of a WWI
bomber—primitive, utterly masculine, mysteriously
functional. The low leather seat gave softly, then cupped
to fit her. Jade stared at the dash in dismay. 'What's

that?' She pointed at a dial.

'The tachometer, chump.' Settling in beside her, Zan suddenly seemed enormous. He closed his door awkwardly.

'They left that off my Volkswagen,' she murmured, stretching her long legs out. Her toe just grazed the brake pedal.

'You'll have to adjust the seat, Jade,' he prompted.

'Where's the lever?'

'I forget. I haven't changed it in three years.'

She glanced at him nervously. 'No one else drives her?'

'Not till now,' Zan said softly. 'You're the first.'

This seemed significant to him, though she couldn't see why. Bringing the seat forward, she fingered the stickshift gingerly. The clutch was surprisingly stiff. She ran through the forward gears once, and then twice again as he watched narrowly.

'Okay, now this is reverse.' Zan shifted awkwardly with his left hand, then made her follow the pattern. 'Now, let's see you back out of here.' He handed her the keys.

Jade bit her lip. His unblinking attention was beginning to unnerve her. She fumbled for the ignition. There wasn't one. She flicked a wary glance at Zan. Was this a joke?

His grin was utterly male, the product of centuries of mechanical superiority. 'Other side, sweet,' he said softly.

'What? Oh!' She stared indignantly at the ignition. Why hide it to the left of the wheel? 'The name is not "sweet", by the way,' she said carefully. The engine throbbed awake with a soft purr.

'No, you're not sweet,' Zan agreed smoothly. 'But if I called you "tart", you'd probably take it wrongly.'

Glaring into his laughing eyes, Jade shifted into reverse and let the clutch out. The Porsche lunged back-

wards, then died with a soft grunt. 'Damn!' she said
feelingly.

'Try it again, Jade, and this time go a little slower and
smoother with the clutch, and give her more gas,' he
advised, settling back with the air of a man prepared to
be patient.

Jade glanced in the rear-view mirror as she started the
engine again. The garage was built into the side of the
landscaped slope above the condominiums, and the
pavement behind the Porsche slanted up to the doorway. It would take some power to back up that narrow
ramp. Faintheartedness would not pay here. She bit her
lip.

'Try it again, *sweet*,' Zan encouraged brightly.

Flicking a savage glance at him, she stamped on the
pedals. Rubber squealing, the Porsche shot backwards
into the sunlight and died.

'*Cripes!*' Zan breathed reverently, pushing himself off
the dash.

Her teeth flashed white as she smiled back at him,
daring him to say a word. Just one.

He rubbed a fist thoughtfully across his lips, his eyes
measuring her glittering green gaze. Gold brows lifted in
a faint shrug. 'Try first,' he said mildly. 'It should be
easier.'

It was. The Porsche pounced forward and kept moving. She had it now. They mounted the rise to the main
road with hardly a hiccup. Jade glanced at him smugly.

'And best of all, I'm insured,' he told her, his eyes
dancing. 'Just keep an eye out for moving stop signs.'

Driving a Volkswagen would never be the same again,
Jade thought wistfully, as she swung the Porsche into the
teeming parking lot of the local supermarket. It was
dangerous to acquire tastes you couldn't afford. Weav-
ing through the traffic, she found an emtpy space and
pulled in, mindful of the gleaming flanks of the sports
car. Zan sighed softly in unconscious relief and straight-

ened his shoulders as the engine shut down. He looked around with the air of a dreamer awakening.

Jade laughed. 'That wasn't so bad, was it?' She was absurdly proud of herself suddenly, eager for praise.

Zan considered her boastful face, a smile tugging at the corners of his straight lips. 'Not bad at all, for a first run. I thought you showed remarkable restraint back there, when we passed that jogger.'

'Brute!' Handing him the keys, she slipped out, and turned to see him grapple with his door. She bit her lip and looked away guiltily.

'Come on, Jade.' Zan's hand closed on her upper arm, sending warm tremors fluttering across her shoulders. 'Your job is to restrain *me*. I can feel a feeding frenzy coming on.' He tugged her along gently, his long legs taking one stride for each two of her steps. 'Don't let me buy more than two cartons of ice cream!'

Jade laughed and glanced ahead at the store windows, and her smile faded. How many times had she and Fred shopped here together, for some meal they were sharing? Or had met here by accident? Why, everyone they knew in town shopped here! She glanced down at the hand on her arm with vague distress, and stopped short. This was all wrong. She stared past Zan's quizzical face towards the entrance, and swallowed hard. She didn't *want* to go shopping with Zan. She shook her head and stepped back, pulling away from him.

'What's the matter, Jade?' His eyes probed her face.

'I . . . have to get something at the pharmacy, Zan,' she managed breathlessly. 'Why don't we just meet at the car?'

He shook his head, his eyes suddenly cold. 'Meet me in the store . . . I'll need help with the bags,' he said curtly. He strode off without her, half a head higher than any man he passed, and she looked after him unhappily.

That was stupid, Jade decided a few minutes later as she stood staring at the shampoos. Shampoos for grey

hair, shampoos for bleached hair, shampoos for dry
hair, and a miracle in every bottle. True love and
happiness for ever, if one only chose the right brand.
Now why had she panicked like that? She wandered
down the pharmacy aisle, contemplating hair products
gloomily. Fred . . . she would have to telegram Fred
tomorrow, and then follow that up with a letter reassur-
ing him that this was just a postponement, not a change
of heart . . . She found herself staring at the creme
rinses, which she was nearly out of, come to think of it.
Too bad, because she hadn't a penny on her.

She stopped, frowning. What *was* she going to do
about money, anyway? Fred had arranged for her to
work as an illustrator and general assistant for the
project, and she'd counted on that to give her pin money
for the summer. If any big expenses had come up, Fred's
salary would have covered them, of course. But now
what would she do? She scowled at the hair sprays.

She'd not got much for selling her VW yesterday, but
it should keep her in groceries and paint for a month at
least. And if she had paints, she could manage for the
rest of the summer, she told herself firmly—if Zan gave
her time to use it, that was. The tourists who jammed
Newport's streets in the summer months had an insati-
able hunger for seascapes. Come to think of it, she'd
better rescue her pet paintings tomorrow, or they'd all
be gone. She moved on.

But would he give her time to paint? He'd certainly
kept her busy enough today. Well, I'll just have to make
time, she decided, Zan or no Zan. He can't write every
minute. In the meantime, it was probably best to
humour him. A happy master was a good master. She
smiled wryly. Three months or one book, whichever
comes first, she promised herself. I can stand it. Rubbing
her thumbs across sore fingertips, she hurried out of the
drugstore.

Jade found Zan amongst the crackers, honey-blond

hair falling in his eyes as he stooped to inspect the boxes. She stopped beside him.

'Find what you need?' he asked idly, his eyes scanning the saltines.

'Er . . . yes.' She'd forgotten her lie already.

Zan's pale eyes swung to her empty hands, and then up to her face. He examined her thoughtfully. 'Oh?'

'Lip-gloss,' she explained, hastily, her hands clenching. That at least would have fitted into the pocket of her shorts.

Zan's eyes moved to her bare lips and lingered there for a long moment and then to her cheeks. 'Floodtide,' he murmured gently, turning back to the crackers. Rubbing a hand across her hot face, Jade scowled at his back. *Damn* the man, anyway.

'Bring the cart over here, Jade,' he commanded, grabbing two boxes in a big hand. He dumped them in, and reached for more. And more.

'You're expecting company, Zan?'

He smiled. 'Nope, I'm just expecting not to waste time shopping. I'd rather write.' He jerked his chin at the cart. 'Why don't you push?'

'All right.'

Zan padded beside her, his restless laser eyes sweeping the shelves and then flicking to the shoppers as they passed by. Two bottles of steak sauce in one hand, he stopped to watch an old man shuffle past with a cart full of cat food.

'Your mother never told you not to stare, Zan?' she teased.

Turning back to her, his eyes were suddenly sorrowful beneath the thick gold lashes. 'I never had a mother, Jade,' he explained bravely. 'I'm an orphan.'

'Oh.' She bit her lip in sympathy. 'I'm sorry, Zan.'

He shot her a contrite glance. 'And I'm a liar, sweet. Pay me no heed. Starvation brings out the worst in me.'

His lips twitched. 'That and wide-eyed girls who believe everything you tell 'em.' He touched her arm to start her moving again, the lines fanning out from his own wide eyes.

Jade scowled. He was impossible! 'Seriously, Zan, why do you watch people like that?'

He reached up to the soy sauce, muscles sliding under the brown skin of his arm. 'I'm a writer, sweet, remember? Where do you think the material comes from?' Wedging two bottles into the cart, he straightened to look down on her. 'In fact, in the novel I'm working on now, there's going to be a heroine with long hair . . .' He reached out to lift a curl of hair off her shoulder, rubbed it slowly between his fingers. 'Hair like a curtain of silk . . .' His eyes danced as they met her horrified gaze. 'And the funny thing is, she thinks it's auburn, while everyone else thinks . . .'

Jade pulled back from his hand, her eyes flashing. Zan didn't let go. Her hair stretched between them, a gleaming leash. 'Don't you dare!' she hissed.

Grinning evilly, he lifted the lock over her shoulder and set it free. 'Try to stop me,' he teased.

'Try to get it typed!' she shot back.

His gold brows jumped. 'That could be a problem,' he conceded. 'In the meantime, come tell me what kind of barbecue sauce you like.' Touching her shoulder, he eased her along the aisle.

'*I* like?' Jade flashed him a wary look. 'Why does that matter?'

'I'm just seeking housewifely advice, sweet. What kind do you feed lover boy?' Zan looked down at her innocently.

Lover boy. Jade shut her eyes and took a deep breath. And another. She couldn't let him get to her like this. She *wouldn't*. She opened her eyes. 'Try the Krafts,' she cooed, her eyes glinting dangerously.

He laughed softly, conceding defeat, and took four

bottles. 'Let's get the meat,' he suggested, 'before I faint dead away.'

In the meat department, he leaned over the steaks hungrily. 'What kind do you usually buy, Jade?'

Her smile was genuine this time, and wry. 'The cheapest, Zan, when I buy them at all. I'm a teacher in a private high school, remember?'

He nodded, his eyes caressing the beef. 'Do you like teaching?'

Jade considered that. 'Do you know the rhyme about the little girl, with the curl in the middle of her forehead? When she was good, she was very, very good, but when she was bad, she was—'

'*Awful*,' he chanted for her, looking up and grinning now. 'What would you rather do?'

'Paint.'

Zan nodded again, his grey eyes serious. 'I want to see your work.'

'I suppose you will, sooner or later.' She looked away from him, suddenly embarrassed.

'Okay,' he announced decisively. 'We've poked around long enough. Let's get moving. Hold out your hands, Jade.' He selected a T-bone and handed it to her, and then another. Flipping through the selection, he chose a third, and a fourth. 'Let's try a few rib eyes,' he suggested, stacking packages into her hands.

Jade wrinkled her nose. 'Stop! That's all I can carry!' Hooking her chin over the top package, she retreated towards their cart.

He was over in the poultry section prodding fryers when she returned. 'Wouldn't it be better to buy them cut up, Zan?' she asked doubtfully. How would he manage with one hand?

But his smile was serene. 'I know what I'm doing, woman. Take this. And this . . .'

She stared down at the mounting packages. 'How big is your freezer?'

'Big.' He brushed the hair off his forehead. 'Now let's get some vegetables. And don't let me forget charcoal, whatever you do.' He touched her arm, urging her onward. Obviously starvation was setting in rapidly. Loading the cart methodically, they rounded the end of the vegetable aisle.

Jade stopped short. 'This is what you need, Zan.' She inspected the potted plant display and chose a begonia in a hanging basket. It was just about to bloom.

But Zan looked sceptical. 'How do you cook 'em?'

'Brute!' She flinched away, hugging the plant to her breast. 'Pay him no heed, baby,' she murmured into its leaves, 'he never means anything he says.' She looked up at him warily. 'You don't have a single plant in your place, Zan.' Reaching up, she brushed his chin with the leaves coaxingly.

His pale eyes regarded her through the foliage. 'I don't have plants for a good reason, Jade. I have a black thumb, and Mona's is brown. And if it survived us, our tenants would no doubt deliver the coup de grâce.' He smiled gently.

She lowered the begonia, and looked down at its soft leaves, suddenly, inexplicably, sad. 'Tenants?'

'The condo's just a summer place, Jade. We'll rent it out for the winters. I don't like the cold. Not for long anyway.' He studied her face, then glanced at the begonia. 'Looks like a healthy little devil,' he murmured judiciously. 'But can you housebreak it?'

'Housebreak it . . .' she looked up indignantly. 'Why, this one will chase burglars and fetch the morning paper!'

His eyes crinkling, Zan took the plant from her and balanced it carefully in the cart, 'Tell you what,' he said lightly, 'we'll buy it for you, and you can loan it to me until September.' He inspected her face sternly. 'But *you* feed it, *you* walk it, and it doesn't sleep on our bed!'

Our bed—the image was utterly unexpected, incredibly vivid. Her lips parted in shock and then anger, Jade spun away from his laughing eyes. Even for a joke, that was outrageous. He was impossible!

Shaking her hair back from her face, she pretended to inspect the eggplants, picked one up at random. Its glossy skin was as cool as her fingers were warm. She was burning up, glowing all over—*sunburn*, she told herself firmly, setting the eggplant down again. She moved on to the Brussels sprouts and then the carrots, fingering the packages intently, taking her time as her cheeks slowly cooled. Another minute and it would be safe to look up again. The jerk! 'Do you want carrots, Zan?' she murmured finally, her eyes downcast.

'Couldn't live without them.' Beside her, he dropped a cucumber into the cart, then moved away again.

Jade stared at the carrots. She would have to get used to Zan's needling. Obviously he was just a joker. As long as she reacted, he would continue to tease. She would just have to learn to keep her cool, that was all. She picked out a bag with small carrots—more likely to be tender—and turned, only to bump into Zan's broad chest as he loomed beside her.

'Did lover boy ever tell you that your eyes turn the colour of fine old romaine when you're angry, Jade?' he murmured huskily, his lips at her ear.

Jade drew a deep, a very deep, breath. *Keep your cool.* If she could handle a class of fourteen-year-old barbarians, surely she could handle *one* overgrown lunatic. Couldn't she? Turning to face him, she opened her eyes and blinked. Their noses were practically touching. His lashes were nearly as long as her own. 'No, I don't believe he ever did, Zan,' she drawled carefully.

Thick eyebrows jumped gently. Below them, his clear eyes gleamed with mischief. 'Well, I don't think I'll tell you that either,' he decided softly. 'You might get mad.' The straight line of his lips quivered as he studied her blazing eyes. 'In the meantime, what's your favourite flavour of ice cream—lime sherbet?'

'Butter almond, and what does it matter?' she snapped, leaning back against his encircling arm. Suddenly she had a splitting headache.

Zan didn't bother to answer that as he let her go, his strange eyes gleaming in satisfaction. 'Fate,' he murmured obscurely, and wandered off towards the frozen dessert section.

Zan was silent on the trip back. Silent with gleaming eyes as they passed a runner, stoically silent when Jade ground the gears shifting down for a stop sign. Golden brows knotted into a thoughtful line, he leaned back, relaxed and blessedly quiet, and let her drive. Jade rolled down a window and let her hair blow, her aching head cooling in the sweet evening breeze. She was just hungry and tired, that was all. She'd help him in with the groceries and then run for it. She'd done her duty for today. She took a deep breath.

They'd missed the sunset. Beyond the fort, the west glowed soft rose fading to lilac as they drove down the hill. Sky and water still held a lingering flash of quicksilver, but the land had lost its light. Buildings across the harbour were etched blue-black and jagged against the pale sky.

Jade let Zan off at the door with the groceries, then drove on to park the car. Returning through the dusk, she stopped to stare out across the harbour, her eyes tracing the lighted arc of the bridge. She sighed, her heart suddenly easy, and stepped inside.

Zan had already ferried the bags to the kitchen. His rough head bent, he stirred something on the counter as ice tinkled. Turning, he held out a glass to her. 'For you, sweet. It's been a long day.' He smiled warmly.

Jade took it automatically and frowned down at the wedge of lime floating in her glass. She should be going now.

'You do drink gin and tonic, don't you, Jade?' he asked huskily. 'It's great for malaria.'

Smiling, she nodded and took a sip. Tart and cold, it sparkled down her throat, bringing a flush of answering warmth. She took another sip—so good! She would drink this and leave. 'Want me to put away the groceries, Zan?' she asked practically.

He shook his head. 'I'll do that, after I get the charcoal started. Why don't you make the salad?'

Her head came up at that. Did he mean . . . ? She studied him nervously. Surely he didn't think she was staying to supper? Looking back at her, his smile was guileless, but above it the pale eyes were suddenly wary. She shook her head decisively. 'No, Zan, I'm not eating here tonight, thank you, if that's what you mean.' It was none too soon to draw a firm line between their business together and her own private life, though the shopping trip had seemed to blur the distinction somehow.

His brows twitched mildly. 'Of course you are. I've worked you hard today and now I'll feed you.' He turned away, as if the matter were settled, and scrounged in a grocery bag.

Jade brushed her hair back angrily. 'Zan—no! I'll feed myself. Later.' She tossed down the rest of her drink, and clicked the glass down on the counter beside him.

'Jade.' His voice had an edge to it now that she hadn't heard before. Zan seemed to hear it too, because he stopped suddenly. Setting out charcoal lighter and matches, he turned to face her, his face elaborately patient. 'Look, Jade, you gave me breakfast this morning. Why can't I give you supper tonight?' He reached out absently to brush a curl off her cheek.

Suddenly she was furious, her temper flaring out of all proportion. 'As I recall it, Zan,' she snapped, 'you *took* breakfast—I didn't *give* it to you. It was blackmail, remember?'

His jaw tightened ominously, and his eyes narrowed

as he took a step towards her. 'All right, Jade—I *took* it,' he snarled. 'And now, by God, you'll take supper from me!' His good hand clenched at his side as if he were fighting the urge to grab and shake her.

'No, I *won't*!' she said deliberately, scowling up at him, her eyes blazing.

And Zan's eyes were like ice, cold and clear in his granite face. They locked with her own, colliding with an almost physical force, and suddenly Jade couldn't have looked away if she'd wanted to. And she didn't. Now was the time to assert herself. She might have to work for Zan, but she was *damned* if she'd let him push her around! She bit her lip, her eyes wide and determined.

But slowly, Zan's face was changing above her as lines crinkled out from the corners of the grey eyes. The line of his lips jumped once, then straightened again. 'You know, Jade, I've warned you twice now. Keep sticking your chin out like that and you're going to get what's coming to you,' he mocked softly.

That was truer than *he*'d ever know, she thought wryly, licking her lips, feeling the tension beginning to ebb between them. 'Well, if you'd sit down when we fight, Zan, I wouldn't have to sprain my neck glaring up at you,' she pointed out, trying to resume her glare. But she'd lost the look somehow.

'Ho, no.' Zan shook his head. 'I'm no fool. You've got me at enough of a disadvantage, already.' Straightening, he rubbed the back of his neck where the knot of the sling rested. His lips quirked up. 'From the way we're fighting, you'd think this was the last steak in the world, Jade, and we're fighting over who will get it, not whether you'll consent to eat some!' He shrugged and turned to pick up the lighter again. 'You're sure you won't share it with me?'

'Quite sure . . . thanks.' She smiled to take the sting out of her refusal.

Stopping at the door to the patio, he smiled back at

her. 'Well, sit down, then. It shouldn't take too long to cook it.' He stepped out into the dark.

'*Zan!* I'm not—' Hissing in frustration, she followed him outside. 'I said I'm *not* having any!'

Squatting over a Hibachi, Zan shook charcoal into it, his left hand awkward and slow. 'I heard you.' He fumbled with the cap of the charcoal lighter, swearing softly. 'Damn it, it's childproof! Jade?' He handed it to her absently, and stood up, towering above her suddenly.

'Here!' She thrust it at him, glowering. There was a catch coming; she could feel it.

He sprayed the fluid blithely over the Hibachi and stepped back, nudging her with him. A match flared, tracing a tiny blazing curve across the dusk. Flames leaped skyward with a soft 'whump.'

'Zan . . .'

Above her, his eyes flamed. Firelight and shadows played across the hard planes of his face, turning it to a wild and reckless mask. The face of a stranger. But the low voice was smooth. 'I heard you, Jade. You don't want any? Fine. But I like my steak cut up, and I'll need you for that.' Turning, he walked inside.

Speechless, she trailed after him. In the kitchen he was stacking the meat by the freezer. She stared at the pile of packages. It would all need cutting up, every bit of it. The *inconsiderate*—she bit her lip. She would *have* to keep her temper. 'Zan, do you have any skewers?' she asked, coming to stand beside him.

'Why?' He flicked a glance at her, his eyebrows bunched.

'I'm going to introduce you to a new dish tonight—shish-kebabs.' She could cut up his meat and go home. Come to think of it, she should chop up all his steaks now, before he froze them.

'Jade.' There was no nonsense left in his low voice as he turned to her. 'Mix yourself a drink, get out of the way, and go sit down. Once I've put this stuff away, I'll make my salad. Then I'll put the steak on. You should be out of here in . . . an hour and a half. Now shoo!' He gave her a gentle shove.

She stalked to the patio door and stood there, glowering out at the night, counting to ten, then twenty, then a hundred . . . A cool, salty breeze lifted her hair, cooling her hot face. The coals in the Hibachi were beginning to glow now as the flames died. She chewed her lip. A fishing boat chugged out the channel, its nets and outriggers webbed black against the darkening sky. Sighing, she turned.

Zan was hacking at a cucumber, his face set. As she watched, half of it rolled off the chopping block. Dropping the knife, Zan dived for it and missed. It hit the floor with a moist thump. 'Damn!' he said fervently.

Jade sighed again. 'Okay, Zan, give.' Stepping forward, she held out her hand.

'Hmm?' He frowned at her.

'Give me the knife, and fix me a drink, will you?'

His grin flashed for a second, then vanished. 'You've got yourself a deal, sweet,' he said casually.

'So, any more wine?' Zan lifted the bottle enquiringly, his eyes smiling.

Jade shook her head lazily. 'I'll just finish what I have, thanks.' She pushed her plate aside and leaned back in her chair, smiling at him sleepily. Her lashes brushed her cheeks for a moment. She was full of good food, good wine, excellent talk, and now she just wanted to float away. It was like being a child again. Someone should pick her up and carry her off to bed . . . A feather-light touch brushed her cheek and her lashes fluttered open. Zan stood beside her.

'Come on, sleepyhead,' he said softly. 'Let's have our coffee by the fire.'

Yawning, she followed him down the three steps into

the living room. He had set their cups and saucers along the raised hearth. She curled up on the nearest sofa and he stretched out at her feet, leaning back against the stone bank, watching her lazily. Behind him, the fire he had started just before they sat down to eat whispered and crackled. Leaping red light silhouetted the sharp lines of his cheek and jaw, gleamed in the edges of his hair.

Through her contentment, a vague uneasiness began to prickle as the coffee roused her. She glanced around. 'This is a beautiful place, Zan. How did you find it?'

'Mona found it. I just meant to rent a house here, while I did my writing on location—as I usually do. She suggested we buy something, use it as we please, and try to turn a profit.' He drank again. 'The girl's got a genius for real estate. So I went along—sight unseen.' His eyes swept the room and returned to her face. 'I'm glad I did.'

And where *was* the charming blonde who should be sitting here in her place? Jade wondered. To wonder was to ask tonight, and she turned to study him. 'Where *is* Mona?'

Zan smiled wryly. 'Off in Europe cavorting—and breaking hearts. All but her own, I hope.' He looked grim for a second. His brows shrugged and he drank again. He glanced up at her. 'And what about Freddie boy? Why is he cavorting in Greece?'

Jade shifted uneasily, disliking the sudden jeer in his voice. It was a disturbing contrast to the warm, easy voice he'd been using all evening. She ignored the tone. 'Fred is assistant supervisor on an archaeological dig, over there. They're affiliated with a university, and some of his best students go along each summer as well. He's been doing it every summer for as long as I've known him.' She sighed softly. At her feet, Zan stirred restlessly, and she set down her coffee cup. 'I ought to be going.'

Warm and slow, his gaze moved across her face. 'Wait

a minute till I finish my coffee, and I'll walk you home.'
He rubbed the back of his neck, stretching again.

But Jade shook her head. 'Not necessary, Zan. It's
safe to walk the streets here at night.'

Zan's eyes gleamed. 'Dawn's the dangerous time,
hmm?'

She scowled as she caught his meaning, then laughed.
'Brute! Will you ever forgive me?'

He shook his head slowly, eyes laughing. 'Never
forgive; never, ever, forget—that's my motto, Jade. But
if you want to *try* to make amends, there's something
you could do.'

'What?'

'Pull this sling over my head. I want to rest my neck a
moment.' Moving across the floor, he leaned back
against the sofa beside her and bowed his head.

Jade started down at his powerful neck and shoulders,
her nerves stirring strangely. Why did he keep remind-
ing her of Jack? They weren't at all alike . . . 'What do
you want me to do, Zan, untie the knot?'

'Then how would I ever tie it back again?' He shook
his head. 'Just lift it over my head, sweet.'

'All right.' She pulled at it tentatively. It was heavy,
with his cast dragging it down. She sat up, sliding her feet
on to the floor on either side of him to brace herself.
'Okay, duck now.' He bowed his head and she slipped
the knot over, her hands grazing his warm silky hair.

'Aah!' Zan straightened and stretched luxuriously,
groaning softly as he rotated his head. 'Thank you,
sweet.' He rubbed the back of his neck again. 'Much
better.'

'It hurts?'

'Doesn't feel too swift,' he admitted, dropping his
hand slowly.

'I'm sorry.' It seemed only natural to reach out and
touch his thick, straight hair, following it slowly down his
neck till it turned crisp and curly.

Zan arched his neck slowly, pressing back against her hand. 'Mmm,' he purred.

Jade put up her other hand and began to massage his shoulders gently. Groaning softly, he moved against her fingers. His pleasure was infectious. A slow, lazy warmth was spreading up her arms, rolling across her body in slow, hot waves. Her fingers tingled with the warm, hard feel of him, and her hands suddenly stopped as her eyes widened. What was she *doing*?

Turning, he laid the cast across her lap. 'What's the matter, sweetheart? Didn't your mother even warn you about massaging strange men's necks?' A smile warmed his low voice now, but his eyes were watchful.

Wide-eyed, trapped, Jade shook her head. 'She must have forgotten that one,' she murmured breathlessly.

'Careless of her.' Zan's voice was like rough velvet now, rasping along her nerves, stirring fear as it had the first time she came here, and with the fear, a nameless anticipation.

He leaned forward, his good hand combing up through her hair to cup the back of her head as he watched her eyes. His fingers whispered gently against her scalp, starting hot shivers tickling down her spine, waking her breasts to quivering attention. 'Jade?'

'Mmm?' Staring into those clear eyes, she was half hypnotised.

'You'll stay the night?' His voice stroked her, lazy and warm with promise.

Jade blinked heavy lashes, trying to break the spell. 'Why?' she murmured. But that wasn't the right response, was it?

Zan was laughing softly, his hand bending her head down so slowly, so inevitably towards his face. He stopped, his lips only inches from her trembling mouth. 'Why? Because it will be as fun as the day has been, sweet.' He leaned forward slowly, and their lips met.

Warm and gentle, his mouth traced the shape of her

lips, exploring them with a slow, searching sureness that set her soft skin quivering and moving to answer his touch. A sweet tingling warmth was spreading out from her mouth, down over her breasts and across her stomach as his hot breath fanned her cheeks.

Zan's hand tightened in her hair, pulling her closer, pressing her soft flesh against his hard hunger. Her own breath was coming now in short, warm gasps. Eyes closed, she could feel her heart pounding in the dark as his lips moved in a quicker rhythm now, no longer questioning, but demanding.

Jade's eyes fluttered open. Againnst her face, Zan was a moving blur of brown skin, hazy gold. She leaned away from the kiss, but he followed her down till her head met the cushion. She gave a soft, hungry moan of pleasure against his mouth, and he groaned darkly and deepened the kiss in reply, bending her head back over his arm.

Slowly Jade shook her head, but Zan moved with her, using the movement to add a new rhythm to the kiss, swinging her face slowly back and forth with the weight of his mouth. Dizzily, she opened her eyes again. This had to stop, and it had to stop now! Any later would be too late.

She found her hands buried in his hair, dragged them across his cheeks and down his neck to wedge them against the wall of his chest. Beneath his warm shirt she could feel his heart slamming urgently as his breath rasped her face. She pushed out, trying to straighten her arms. There was a brief check in his rhythm, but then the arm around her shoulders tightened and the kiss pressed on. Jade pushed again. The rhythm slowed, and then his mouth stilled against hers. His lashes grazed her cheek as his eyes opened.

Fighting the urge to pull him closer, she pushed instead. Zan sighed against her face, finished the kiss with gentle deliberation, and broke it to lean his forehead against her brow.

Too close to focus on, his grey eyes were a blur. Their lashes tangled as she blinked. His good arm was wrapped around her waist now, holding her close.

He sighed again. 'Fun's not a good enough reason, hmm?' he asked huskily. There was a note of laughter in the breathless voice, as if he'd run a long way to be amused by her.

Jade tilted her head back to see his face. She was too shaken to form an answer, much less say it yet. She shook her head wordlessly, her hair fanning out in a soft sheen across her shoulders. No, fun was not enough . . . not for her anyway . . .

Zan's hand tightened on her waist, not pulling her towards him, but simply feeling her. 'Reasons!' he murmured in exasperation. His lips twitched in a faint smile that was ironic, or rueful, or both. 'I guess maybe I should have said, because I love you madly. But you probably wouldn't have bought that, would you?'

She shook her head again, smiling in spite of herself.

Zan's hand travelled slowly up to trace her spine in an absent, melting caress. His brows knotted. 'Or I suppose I could have said you should stay because I planned to write some more tonight. But I'd rather lie with you than to you.' His hand cupped the back of her head again, urging her forward, then slowly relaxed as she leaned away from the pressure. He sighed. 'I suppose I am rushing things a bit, aren't I?' He murmured, smiling ruefully, but his eyes sharpened as she shook her head slowly. 'No? Then—'

'No, Zan,' she whispered. 'It's not too early . . . It's too late.'

'I doubt if it's past twelve.'

'That's not what I mean and you know it!'

Zan's lips twisted. 'Okay, Jade,' he nodded ironically, 'it *is* late. Let's get you home.'

'You don't have to—'

'Oh, but I *want* to,' he cut in savagely. He stared at her

for a second and then stood up. 'Find your shoes and let's go.'

'What about your sling?' She didn't want the evening to end this way. She stared up at him, hurt and suddenly resentful of his anger. Had he really thought she'd tumble into his bed, just like that? Was that the usual reaction he got from women? Most likely it was, she decided wryly. Well, she'd had experience of that kind of man once before, and once had been enough to last a lifetime! Let the other women stand in line, if they hadn't more sense. She had.

Zan was struggling into his sling already. 'I can manage, thanks.' The anger had passed, or had been suppressed. His voice was brisk, utterly neutral as he turned away.

They walked back through the dark streets in silence, each alone with their thoughts. Their shoulders brushed occasionally, but Zan made no move to touch her, and Jade was grateful. What had got into her back there? What crazy impulse born of firelight, and wine, and Zan's charm, had made her act that way? It was as if the whole evening had conspired to seduce her. It had been like a dream, a golden, hazy moment stolen out of the pattern of her life and her future. And it would be silly to feel guilt for it, as silly and useless as regretting a dream. Already it seemed as if it had happened to some other person, she thought, as the night air cooled her face. *Forget it. It won't happen again.*

Zan's hand closed on her arm as he stopped her at an intersection. Lights swept across them and a car roared by, filled with drunken laughter, running the stop sign. Zan swore softly and hustled her across the street, then dropped her arm again.

Jade glanced up at him. But did Zan realise that tonight was an accident and would never be repeated? He was frowning thoughtfully, his keen eyes scanning the sidewalk ahead, his long strides slow to match her pace. He glanced down at her, then back over his shoulder with street-wise wariness before turning ahead again. It would be awkward if Zan didn't, wouldn't understand. She sighed. He flicked another look at her, and put his hand to her waist to turn her into her own street. Jade took a quick step forward and his hand dropped away. Well, she would make him understand, if necessary. He might not take his relationship with Mona seriously—he didn't take much seriously, come to think of it—but she did hers with Fred. She was not going to change her life and her loyalty for one night of 'fun', as Zan had put it . . . That might be her mother's style, but it would not be hers . . . Fun as it might have been . . .

Zan's hand pulled her back. 'Whoa, where are you going, Jade?'

She looked up. He was right, she'd nearly walked past her own door. She shook her head ruefully. 'Well, Zan . . .'

But he was tramping up her squeaky steps already to wait on the porch. She followed him up warily, digging her keys from her pocket. 'Thanks for walking—'

'Let's make sure no one's inside first, Jade. Why don't you lock this door?' he broke in irritably.

'It hasn't been locked in years, since there's two apartments here. The top door's my front door really.'

He opened the door for her and followed her inside. 'Who lives on the first floor?'

'No one. It's uninhabitable, right now. It was damaged in a fire—just before I bought the house.' Would he never leave? She turned and started up the stairs and he followed. At her door, she turned to face him, her face set with determination. 'Goodnight, Zan.'

He studied her silently for a moment, his brows bunched in a shaggy, puzzled line. 'See you at eight-thirty,' he said at last.

'Eight-thirty? I've got some errands to do!'

Zan shook his head firmly. 'I like to start early, and

that *was* part of the deal, Jade. You agreed to be there when I . . . want . . . you, day or night.' His lips twitched as she shuddered, reacting to the twist he had put on the word, and his hand reached out, his thumb brushing her bottom lip in a butterfly caress. He smiled as her chin jerked angrily. 'So goodnight, sweet. I'll see you at eight-thirty.' He turned and went down the stairs, moving lightly for so big a man.

Jade stared after him, eyes wide as the door closed gently. Now she knew why Zan reminded her of Jack. He wasn't really like her first lying love at all. It was something inside *her*. Somehow Zan struck the same response, like a careless finger brushing across a guitar string. She shivered. 'Fred?' she called softly. Silence . . . her own voice sounding hollow and small in the empty stairwell. Jade shuddered again and stepped inside, wandered slowly across to the plants above the sink. She pulled a sprig of mint and crushed the leaf under her nose—a kindly, friendly smell. Fred . . .

CHAPTER FIVE

'"And the dark folded around him like sleep, like a blanket tucked round his shoulders by loving hands."'

Zan paused, and Jade dropped her hands into her lap. Something in his tone, or maybe the words themselves, told her that this was the end of the chapter, this last delusion of a stunned and dying man. She shuddered and then leaped as a hand found her shoulder. 'Oh!'

Inches from her ear, Zan chortled evilly. 'May all my readers react thus, Jade!' Leaning above her, he scanned the page.

Jade read it over again with him, squinting in the near twilight. It was hard to follow the plot and type at the same time, but in re-reading it, she was impressed. It wasn't her kind of story, but Zan's words had a kind of power, a sardonic, almost poetic vision of blood and death. Suddenly conscious of the hand on her shoulder, she looked up, bumping his jaw with her forehead—he was that close. She ducked, turning to study the page again, her nostrils flaring with the scent of him—sunshine and aftershave, and man—a nice combination.

Zan straightened and removed his hand casually. 'We'll call that a day, Jade,' he said quietly, satisfaction obvious in his low voice. A productive afternoon had followed a morning in which nothing had satisfied him on this second day of their collaboration.

Jade turned to look up at him again. 'This is really rather good, Zan,' she said seriously. 'I'm impressed.'

His lips twitched upwards in his grave face. 'Why, thank you, ma'am. Such praise is rain in the desert of a hack writer's ego.' He glanced at the table. 'We'd better get this inside before the dew falls, sweet.'

Pulling the last sheet from the typewriter, Jade gathered the manuscript together. 'My room-mate in college was a mystery addict, but I don't remember ever seeing your name in Liz's collection. Were you writing four years ago?'

Zan scooped up the typewriter carefully. 'Yes, child, I was,' he answered, his voice dry. 'But there are such things as pen-names.' He turned towards the glass doors.

'Oh, right. What's yours—Gore Alexander?' she teased.

'Wyk Halloran,' he told her and drifted inside.

Jade froze, staring down at the table. Wyk Halloran . . . rather good, she'd told him! She could feel the blush climbing all the way from her waist. Half of America thought Wyk Halloran was rather good, or rather better than good, judging from the best-seller lists these last few years. She'd never read him herself. Zan must be inside, bent double just now with her naïve compliment!

Jade's head snapped up. Or was this his idea of a joke? Truth ran a poor second to a good story every time in Zan's world, she was learning. Was this just another of his pranks? She wandered inside warily, her eyes narrowed.

Ice tinkled in the kitchen. Zan was mixing drinks. Damn! She hadn't meant to drink with him tonight, nor eat with him, for that matter. She studied his bent head, still feeling like a fool. Was this a put-on or was it not? H as in Hubert, he'd said at the hospital—but not Hubert. Wyk as in Wykoff, obviously.

Zan dropped a lime into each glass, and brought one to her. 'That's confidential, by the way,' he said quietly. He turned back to collect his own glass, avoiding her eyes as if he were the embarrassed one. 'What will it be tonight, Jade? Steak or barbecue chicken?' He glanced up at her quizzically, eyes widening in anticipation. 'I just happen to have your favourite barbecue sauce on hand . . .'

But struggling to reconcile her lunatic blackmailer with the famous writer, Jade was too preoccupied to rise to his bait. It was like seeing double. Which was the real man? She shook her head absently. 'Neither for me, thanks, Zan. You take the chicken, and I'll cut it into parts before I leave.'

Zan shook his head briskly. 'I've got some letters for you to type after supper, Jade. Stick around.' Collecting matches and lighter, he stepped out into the dusk again.

Frowning, Jade leaned in the doorway, sipping her drink. And did he really mean to work, or was this just another line? She wasn't in the mood for a wrestling match tonight, with either a famous writer or a practical joker.

Zan loomed above her, blocking out the lights of the harbour and the bridge beyond. He studied her angry face, his head cocked. 'You're not hungry?' he asked softly.

She shrugged moodily.

'Or you're tired of typing?' he suggested.

Jade looked down at her drink, ignoring him.

'Or let's see . . .' Zan considered. 'It's crossed your mind that I'll go berserk again tonight, when the moon rises—could that be it?' There was laughter in the low voice, and Jade smiled in spite of herself, her face hidden.

A warm hand closed on her chin, bringing her face up. 'Or maybe—just *maybe*,' he mused lightly, 'you're afraid that you'll enjoy it if I do . . . go berserk.' His brows twitched gently as he watched her face freeze.

'Is that what happens when you become famous, Zan?' she drawled evenly, 'You become irresistible to women? I never thought fatheads were very attractive, myself.'

Zan grinned. 'The lady has *teeth*,' he murmured ruefully. 'Is it safe to let you go?'

'Safest.' She glowered up at him.

'Okay.' He dropped her chin gingerly and moved his hand back out of reach. 'Anyway, whatever the reasons for your reluctance, I will behave,' he said lightly, '. . . if you'll make the salad.'

'A deal,' she nodded, and turned away, her heart pattering its own light, strange dance.

'You barbecue a mean chicken, Zan.' Jade licked a finger with a cat-like flick, and leaned back lazily to watch him eat.

'I've found they're usually tenderer than nice chickens,' he answered absently, serving himself more salad. He had an appetite to match his size, she'd noticed. 'And my father always told me that the way to a woman's heart was through her stomach. Have another drumstick, by the way.' He waved the plate under her nose.

She shook her head, smiling. 'No, thanks.'

Zan rubbed his chin thoughtfully, his hair falling softly down towards his eyes. 'I never thought about it before, but I wonder if the corollary is true? Do women without stomachs have hearts at all?' His laser eyes fastened on her flat stomach and travelled leisurely upwards to study her left breast with scientific detachment.

Strange how he could heat her blood with just a look. She held herself utterly still beneath the caress, willing the blush to stay down. Which of course brought it on faster. She looked up in warm defeat to find him grinning faintly. 'Tell me about your father,' she said hastily. 'Is he still alive?'

'And kicking.' Zan's lips curled at some private memory. 'There's not much to tell really. He's president of a tiny private college down in Maryland, has been since I was a kid. Has two passions in life—my mother and fishing.' His eyes mused.

'And your mother?'

'A pretty lady. Looks like porcelain, bounces like a basketball. Two passions in life—Dad and writing poetry.' He pushed his plate aside.

'Is she good?' So that was where he got his way with words.

Zan looked up, eyes devilish. 'You know, I've often wondered myself, but I've never had the nerve to ask Dad. He still packs a good punch.' He laughed openly at the face she made.

'Lout! Your own mother! I meant her poetry, not in bed!'

His smile faded gently. 'Very, very good.' He stood up. 'Butter almond or chocolate chip ice-cream?'

'Neither, Zan. I'm full!'

'Spoilsport!' he taunted. 'Coffee, then. Think it's warm enough to have it on the patio?'

'Just barely.'

'Fix it and I'll be down in a minute.' He headed upstairs.

A soft, damp breeze still ruffled the harbour, and the lights of the town flickered and blinked in the black waters. The sails of a small boat gliding past caught the light like a moon on moth wings—a flicker of white and then gone. Jade leaned out against the wall, shivering slightly.

'Here.' Zan draped something warm over her shoulders and attempted to wrap it around her. 'This perishing cast!' he growled.

Jade finished shrugging it on. It was a sweater, enormous and warm, smelling faintly of Zan. She hugged it closer. 'Thanks, Zan.'

Beside her, Zan cursed softly as he struggled to wriggle into another sweater.

'Be still!' Jade commanded. Laughing at his disgust, she reached up to help him. Tiptoeing to wrap the right side around his shoulder, she tucked the empty sleeve into his sling. When she looked up, she found his face at her hair, and turned away quickly, her heart lurching. 'Let's see. Here's your coffee, Zan.' It sloshed over as she thrust the cup at him.

'Thanks.' He really *could* smile with his voice. Shoulder to shoulder they stared out at the reflections, their arms bumping occasionally as they drank.

Turning his back on the harbour at last, Zan eased up to sit on the wall. He studied her silently. 'So tell me about lover boy,' he said finally.

Irritation flicked through Jade's happiness like a cold draught of wind and she frowned up at him. Why did he have to break the mood like this? 'His name is Fred, thanks,' she said deliberately, 'and I wish you'd remember that.'

'Fred who?'

'Waring. And that's all I care to say,' she said firmly, her chin coming up. She absolutely refused to lay out her relationship with Fred for Zan's entertainment. That would simply give him more ammunition for the next day's teasing. Jade studied his watchful face. There was also something in his manner that disturbed her, some feeling she got that his mocking interest masked something else again. Hostility? But why?

Zan's eyes glittered in the moonlight. 'Not talking, hmm? That's no fun.' He rubbed his chin. 'Why don't we trade, then?'

'Trade what?' she asked suspiciously.

'I'll tell you about my blue-eyed Arabian sweetheart, and you tell me about Fred.'

'No, thanks.' She brushed her hair back disdainfully.

Zan looked like a small boy culling through his baseball cards. He looked up. 'What if I throw in my one-legged Frenchwoman?' he coaxed, eyes gleaming.

'Forget it!' She finished her coffee to hide her smile.

He sighed. 'You're tough, Jade . . . Okay.' He hesitated, measuring her resistance. 'Suppose . . . I tell you the truth about the three-day, bring-your-own-condiment orgy on St John's?' He waited hopefully, gold brows high and shaggy.

Jade considered, prolonging his suspense. She looked up. 'What condiment did you bring, Zan?'

'Mango chutney,' he said gravely.

'Chutney?' She wrinkled her nose and shook her head quickly. 'Now, if you'd said crunchy peanut butter . . .'

'Oh, well, maybe it was peanut butter, now that I think of—'

'*No*, thank you.' Jade gathered up her cup and saucer. She suddenly had no desire to hear about Zan's loves and misadventures, imaginary or otherwise. None at all, she told herself firmly.

Reaching out, he snagged her left wrist, his face almost serious. 'So just answer me one question?'

'Let go!' She pulled back, suddenly angry. His strength still frightened her. But the warm, gentle grip only tightened a fraction. 'You said you'd behave, Zan!'

'It's all relative,' he smiled faintly. 'This *is* behaving, for me, Jade. I'll show you the difference, if you like,' he offered hopefully, pulling her closer.

Jade gave a final yank and then stood still, head thrown back in anger. 'No, thanks,' she said bitterly.

'Just one question. Then I'll answer you one,' Zan coaxed, his thumb caressing her pulse point.

'What's your question?' she scowled, shaking her hair back again.

'How long have you worn this?' He gave her hand a gentle flip and the tiny diamond winked in the moon-light.

She stared up at him, trying to judge the intent of his curiosity, but could find none. 'Two months,' she growled softly.

'And how long have you known him?'

But Jade shook her head. 'That's a second question.'

'So it is,' he agreed serenely, pulling her closer, and his eyes crinkled as she hurried to answer.

'Three years!'

'Aaah . . .' Zan released her gently, smiling his satisfaction.

'What do you mean, "aaah"?' She glowered up at him.

He looked like the cat with the canary feathers on his chin. 'Just "ah".' His smile widened. 'And your question?'

'Thanks, but there isn't one damn thing I care to know about you, Zan.' She turned and stalked inside, her head high.

She glared around, searching for her shoes, hugging the sweater to her. Turning towards the patio, she found Zan leaning in the doorway.

'Where do you think you're going?' he asked warily.

'Home!' she snapped. 'I do have a home, you know, Zan, and just a few things to do there.' She whirled away. Where were her wretched shoes?

'We've got some letters to type first.' He slid the patio door shut and began to pull the curtains.

'Then let's do them!' Jade rapped the typewriter down on the table and laid out the paper. 'I haven't got all night.' Furious and not even sure why now, she turned to scowl at him, her eyes blazing.

'I'm thinking,' he said patiently. 'If you're in such a tearing hurry, run up and find my address book. It's on the bureau in my room.' Sitting down, he leaned back in his chair and stared moodily at the ceiling.

Jade skittered up the stairs and into his room, flipping on the light. The bureau was large, more a desk than a bureau, and cluttered. She stared at the piles of books, searching for an address book. A small red notebook caught her eye and she flipped it open. 'Harry Granger,' she read, and then an address. In parentheses below that, Zan had 'grandchildren (3) and canaries'. Mystified, Jade blinked at this cryptic notation.

She flipped a page. John Hudson was followed by golf, New York Yankees, and rum and Coke. Amused, she turned the page again. These were the notes of a busy man, considerate enough, or clever enough, to want to keep track of his friends' interests and preferences. 'Sheila Mallow,' she read. 'Gardenias and Italian food.' Jade's smile widened. Lindy Pierson liked 'Joy perfume and foreign films.' Diana Tallon was 'roses and incredibly ticklish,' according to Zan. Wanda Thayer . . . Jade shut the book with a snap, suddenly not amused any more. Taking it, she wandered around the balcony to the bathroom to inspect her hair.

She looked like a waif tonight in Zan's old sweater— eyes big and sad, hair windblown, cheeks flushed. Her nose would start peeling tomorrow. She glanced down at the book in her hands. And what did Mona like? Zan and real estate and old silver? She didn't even know Mona's last name to look her up and find out. A surge of sympathy welled up in her, as she thought of the laughing blonde. It must be dreadful to love Zan, really love him. Obviously, from the sheer quantity of women here in this book, he didn't take his loves any more seriously than he did anything else in his life. But then maybe Mona was the same sort. Maybe they were a good match—two devastatingly attractive, light hearted, light-loving people, skimming the surface, never stopping to feel deeply. No doubt life was gayer and simpler that way.

'Jade?' Zan shouted from down below.

Jade shivered and brushed her hair back. 'Coming, Master!'

'I'll just lie down for a minute,' Jade decided, studying the mattress on the newly-mopped kitchen floor with wistful reddened eyes. Her knees started to buckle, but she straightened them abruptly and leaned back against the kitchen counter instead. If she lay down now, she'd never get up again. Yawning hugely, she glanced slowly around the room. She was standing in the kitchen of the downstairs apartment of her own house. This room and the bathroom next to it would be home for the rest of the summer.

Above her head, she could hear the light footsteps of her summer tenant as she moved into the second floor apartment. It had been too late to cancel Cathy Kenyon's lease, by the time Zan changed Jade's summer plans for her. She grimaced, and it changed into a yawn again. Besides, she needed the money. The girl's rent would almost cover the mortgage payments.

Jade glanced around the kitchen again. The smoke-stained, streaky walls looked unbearably shabby, but, compared with its sooty condition of two days ago, the room was a miracle of cleanliness—all vacuumed and washed down and ready for painting. Later, when she found the time, she would paint the walls white and then would tackle the smoke-damaged front rooms of the apartment. It had been all she could do, this last week, just to scrub these two rooms and move out from upstairs, what with Zan demanding almost every waking minute of her days. She'd stayed up till dawn the night before last, and last night, she'd simply not gone to bed at all in her frenzy to finish the job. No doubt her half-holiday today was due to the shadows under her eyes that Zan had noticed yesterday.

That reminded her, and she blinked at her watch wearily, she was due at the condominium in half an hour. She should get moving. But it was easier to just slouch where she was, and she looked around the room one last time with sleepy satisfaction. Grubby as it was, it was nice to have a hidey-hole that Zan didn't know about. She didn't mean to tell him either. And she had instructed a wide-eyed, puzzled Cathy to say—if she was ever asked—that Jade had moved away to address unknown in early June. It was a silly impulse, no doubt, but somehow she wanted to preserve this scrap of independence, this last privacy from Zan if she could . . . He was such a tyrant. Speaking of tyrants . . . Jade pushed off the counter and then stood still for a moment as the floor tilted and then levelled again. Lord, she was tired!

Zan looked up from the sofa as she entered the condominium, then glanced at his watch pointedly. 'You're late, Jade.'

'Yes,' Jade nodded absently. The short walk over had finished her. She wondered if she'd even be able to *see* the typewriter keys, much less hit them. And there were hours left in the day, hours until she could lie down and sleep.

'Come sit down,' Zan commanded, patting the cushion beside him.

But Jade sank into a seat across the pit from him instead. He still made her nervous sometimes, especially when his eyes narrowed to that laser beam look, as they were doing right now. She smiled brightly and waited for his scolding. When it didn't come, she relaxed, sagging slowly back into the cushions, her lashes drooping. She blinked, then jerked awake as the sofa dipped under Zan's weight. He leaned over her, studying her face carefully. She turned her head away, but a big hand caught her chin and swung her back for inspection.

'You look like you've been crying all night, with those red eyes, Red,' he remarked casually. 'Something on your conscience?'

Jade shut her eyes and shook her head, too tired to attempt an explanation.

'Did you hear from lover boy?' he probed.

Frowning at the label, she held her tongue, her eyes still closed. It was too soon to expect a letter yet.

'Or maybe you haven't heard from the skunk, is that the problem?' he asked whimsically. 'Hmm?'

It was easier to let Zan find his own explanations, Jade

decided, than to find a lie that would satisfy him, since she didn't mean to tell him the truth. She hid in the dark, enjoying the unexpected gentleness of his hand and voice.

He released her, and fabric rustled nearby. 'Well, one thing's certain,' he remarked, 'you're no good to me like this.'

A hard arm slid behind her shoulders, something much harder beneath her knees, and her eyes flashed open. 'Zan!' She grabbed at his neck as the ground fell away.

'Sit still,' he chided gently. 'I don't want to drop you.' He turned towards the stairs.

'Put me down!' She gasped up into his face. 'You'll hurt your arm!'

His long lips twitched just above her. 'Only if you keep wiggling, sweet. I'm not carrying you with my wrist, if you give me the choice.' He was climbing the stairs now, his easy breathing belying the beat of his heart where her breast rested. His arms tightened for a second, then eased again, slowly.

Why fight him? Jade closed her eyes, her cheek on his shoulder, and let a slow, lazy tide float her away. This was heaven, so safe, so warm. Her eyes fluttered open as the bed sank beneath her. White walls . . . She looked up into Zan's face, her lips parted in sudden alarm. His room, not the guest room . . .

'The view's the finest in the house,' he assured her patiently. 'And no strings attached, sweet. Daydreams for me, maybe. Strings for you, no.' He sat back, looking down at her. 'Now slide out of your clothes and go to sleep, and I'll see you when you wake up.'

She shook her head, her fringed eyes wide with sleepy fright.

Zan smiled crookedly and his hand reached out to smooth her hair off her cheek. 'I'm not coming back to bother you, if that's what you're thinking, Jade,' he said softly. 'I like my women awake.' Leaning down slowly, he took her mouth in a warm, gentle kiss, and as her eyes fluttered and closed, she seemed to sink down beneath it—down, down into the pillow in warm, echoing waves of sleep and pleasure. Dream and waking were all one.

The kiss stopped, leaving her lips quivering for more. 'Nope,' he laughed huskily, just above her. 'That's all you get, not matter how you beg.' His knuckles brushed her bottom lip. 'Now can you undress yourself, sweet?'

Eyes shut, she nodded dreamily.

'Okay,' he said doubtfully. The bed rebounded, the door shut, and she slept.

Smiling, Jade woke and opened her eyes. Her mind peaceful and clear, she savoured the light in the room. Somewhere nearby, the sun must be shining. Reflections of water rippled slowly across the ceiling. Her eyes widened and she sat up. White walls, heaps of books— Zan's room. She stared around quickly, but the door was shut. She was alone.

She sank slowly back on the pillows, breathing deeply. What day was it? She looked towards the glass wall. From the angle of the light across the harbour, it must be morning. So she'd slept the clock around, then. She stretched luxuriously, and smiled again suddenly. She felt marvellous, as if her body still remembered some lovely dream that had just escaped her memory. She threw the covers back and swung her long legs off the bed.

She looked down at herself. Oh—oh! She'd slept in her clothes after all. Zan's question came back to her, and with it, his kiss. She sat still, feeling the blush sweep through her like a wave of heat. Slowly she lay back to stare up at the ceiling. Fred. Remember Fred? she asked herself wryly. The man you decided you could build a kind and loving life with? The kind of love you thought your parents had? She shook her head angrily. This was ridiculous! She couldn't, *wouldn't* let Zan disturb her like this. Not a joker like Zan. She sat up again briskly. A nice cool shower and coffee, that was what she needed. That had some common sense. She padded out of Zan's room, smiling no longer.

Jade was reaching for the handle to the bathroom door when it swung open, and Zan stopped short in the doorway, clouds of steam wafting up around his naked shoulders. Except for his right arm, the rest of him was just as bare. Paralysed, Jade stood there slowly drinking him in—damp, hard brown skin; pale gold hair hazing his chest, curling down in a line across his flat stomach to spread again across his trim loins and his hard thighs. Two parts Greek god, one part teddy-bear. She squinched her eyes shut, blushing so furiously she was almost faint with it.

In the darkness beyond her eyelids, Zan chortled softly. 'Didn't your mother ever tell you not to stare at strangers, little girl?'

'I'm . . . writing a book,' she managed faintly. 'Where do you think the material comes from?'

He laughed again and she heard him move. She flinched as his hand slid into her hair, pulling her head back. 'Damn it, you slept in your clothes after all, Jade,' he murmured huskily, just above her. 'I'll have to find you something of Mona's to wear, I suppose.'

Eyes blazing open, she twisted out of his hold just as his lips brushed her chin. Her hair snagged in his fingers, bringing tears to her eyes, but with a toss of her head she yanked free. Spinning past him into the bathroom, she slammed the door between them, and leaned back against it, her eyes suddenly full of tears. Damn him! Damn, damn, oh, *damn* him!

Beyond the door, there was silence and then, perhaps, a low snort. Soft, slow footfalls told her when he padded away at last.

CHAPTER SIX

WORKING with her finest brush, Jade stroked in the shape of a mast here, just the suggestion of rigging on a boat there, a bright dot for a lobsterpot in the distance. She swished her brush in the can of water and leaned back to study the painting . . . Not bad. Not bad at all, really. It would certainly sell.

She looked out at the harbour again. The view from Zan's guest room balcony wasn't bad, either. Stunning might be even a better description. The only problem was that she'd been painting that same view for two weeks now, whenever Zan wasn't using her. She was ready for a change.

'Red?' Zan's voice came from below, and Jade let out a little hiss of exasperation. Sticking a bare foot over the balcony, she wiggled it derisively.

'Jade?' he tried.

'Yes, Master?' She leaned over to see Zan on the patio below. 'Has inspiration struck yet?' she mocked.

Head thrown back, Zan squinted up at her. 'Nope, I'm one big blank today.' He smiled ruefully. 'I think we're going stale here.'

Nodding in agreement, Jade studied his golden head. Two weeks of pacing in the sun had bleached streaks of silver through the honey colour, and his tan was terrific.

'So, can I go home now, if you're not going to write?' She had made almost no progress at all on her downstairs apartment. The door to the living room and the front entrance was still sealed off to keep the soot out.

But Zan shook his head slowly, frowning. 'Stick around, sweet. I may need you yet.'

Jade scowled down at him, recalling belatedly that she

was not speaking to him today. On a silly impulse, she had worn a light, gauze sundress this morning, instead of her usual shorts, and Zan had been fascinated, had teased her unmercifully. They had spent more time bickering than they had writing, and finally she had retreated to the balcony to paint. In the meantime, he still had the clip he had snitched out of her hair, she thought wrathfully, brushing a fluttering lock back from her eyes as she frowned down at him.

Zan studied her face with amusement. 'What if it gets stuck like that some day?' he teased. 'What would you do then?'

Jade shrugged haughtily, trying to sustain the scowl, but beginning to lose it.

His grin widened. 'I guess it wouldn't be too dreadful,' he decided. 'You're always sexiest when you're angry.'

Jade ducked back out of sight before she smiled and leaned back in her chair. It was best not to let him get started like that. Trouble usually followed. And when would Mona return? she wondered for the fiftieth time. Zan obviously needed a woman—and right now she was the only one in sight.

More importantly, when would she hear from Fred? she wondered. He must have got her first letter a week ago. She should be getting one in return any day now. She sighed. She'd not been very specific in her own letter—mentioning a debt incurred, the need to repay it, and little else. She hadn't really tried to describe Zan. Fred was patient and understanding, but Zan surpassed most normal people's understanding—to say nothing of their patience.

An apple shot up into the air just past the balcony, hovered, and dropped straight down again. Jade's head swung around. Again it floated into view and vanished. She edged closer to the railing. The apple bobbed up for the third time and she nabbed it, laughing in spite of herself. She looked over the railing.

'Oh! Would you like an apple?' Zan looked surprised.

Silently, Jade shook her head. Reaching out, she tried to drop it on his head, but he caught it easily. He was getting good with that left hand.

Zan took a bite, watching her lazily. 'I'm going next door to see Jerry for a few minutes, Jade. I'll be back.'

'Well, don't hurry on *my* account,' she broke her silence to coo sarcastically. 'I just *love* cooling my heels here!'

Jerry was a retired lawyer. Zan and he could discuss the finer points of criminal law and criminals for hours, if not days, on end.

Zan's eyes gleamed. 'Well, if you want to keep your wandering boy at home, you know all it takes, Red.'

Jade smiled sweetly, batting her lashes. 'I guess Jerry has more to offer you, on second thoughts!'

Zan's lips quirked. 'You said it, I didn't.' Disdaining the front door, he ambled over to the corner wall and swung over it on to the boulders below, then strode out of sight around the corner of the condo.

Sighing, Jade stepped off the balcony. It looked like a slow afternoon. Time for a cool drink.

She was just pouring it when the phone rang. Her hand jerked, splashing soda across the counter top. No one ever called them. She had to look twice to even find the phone at the end of the counter nearest the dining room. 'Hello?'

There was a long instant of silence. 'Hello. Who is *this*, please?' The throaty, feminine voice started the question smoothly, but it ended with a bit of steel showing.

Jade eyed the mouthpiece doubtfully. Now who could this be? Mona? Or someone else? It didn't sound like an overseas call. She frowned. Somehow she didn't feel like explaining herself, whatever this woman's rights to an explanation might be. Let her ask Zan.

'Hello? Hello!' The voice had a definite bite to it now.

'Yes? Can I help you?' Jade said briskly, ignoring the previous question.

'Yes,' the woman clipped out. 'Let me speak to Zan, please.'

Zan—not Alexander. So she was a friend. 'I'm afraid he's not in right now, but—'

'When will he be back?' the woman cut in.

'I'm not sure. Could I have him call you when he returns?' Jade kept her voice determinedly neutral.

'No . . .' the voice breathed thoughtfully. 'No, I'll call *him* back later.' There was a note almost of threat in that. For Zan or for me? Jade wondered.

'Fine. Can I tell him who called, please?' She was suddenly depressed. She just wanted to end this.

'Just tell him . . . er . . . that an old lover called.' The woman chuckled nastily as she set the receiver down with a decided click.

Jade put the phone down thoughtfully. An old lover— so there was the end result of loving Zan in a nutshell, right there—jealously. How many women had loved and lost him? How much did it hurt when his interest shifted? Lighthearted, light-loving Zan, spreading jealousy and hurt behind him as he went on his merry, independent way. She shivered. *No, thanks!*

While she waited for Zan, Jade painted a study of the Newport Bridge—abstract, washy, and very blue. Not bad, she decided finally, though rather a departure from her usual style. She finished it and stood up, stretching hugely, to glance at the lowering sun. To heck with him! He could eat supper by himself, for a change.

Gathering the materials off her work table, she brought them inside and set them on the newspaper-covered bureau. The guest room had become her studio—a private lair, a refuge from his teasing and his tyrannies, where Zan was not allowed. Pulling on her hat, Jade slipped into her shoes and hurried downstairs, suddenly anxious to escape.

But she opened the front door to find Zan standing there, reading his mail. Looking up from beneath gold lashes, he studied her casually, then stepped inside, closing the door with a decided thump behind him. 'Where were you going?'

'Home.' She stood her ground defiantly.

'Nope.' Zan tugged the hat down over her eyes and walked past her, putting his arm across her waist as he did so, and kept walking. Jade found herself being walked blindly backwards towards the kitchen.

'Zan, cut it out! I want to go home!' She grabbed hold of his wide shoulder to keep from falling and shook the hat off.

He looked down at her reproachfully. 'Go home now and you'll shatter all the romantic illusions of a fine old gentleman. You're not that cruel, Jade.'

She twisted free of his hold and retreated before him towards the kitchen. 'What are you talking about?'

'Jerry thinks the reason that we're holed up here all day every day is that we're honeymooning.' His cool eyes measured her, waiting for the reaction.

'*Zan!*' Sudden tears of rage welled in her eyes. 'This is a *small town*, you jerk! I'll have to live here when you're gone!' And that kind of rumour she and Fred could live without!

Zan's head jerked up and then stilled, as the mischief faded from his eyes. Thoughtfully, he studied her for a moment. 'Right,' he murmured finally, rubbing a fist across his lips, 'I'll tell him.' He smiled lopsidedly. 'Sorry.'

Her anger was fading as rapidly as it had come. 'Please *do*,' she muttered stiffly. 'Now what did you want done?'

Zan lounged back against the refrigerator, his eyes still inspecting her face. 'Jerry told me a few things that were interesting. I just might get a book out of it some day. Why don't we take out a steak to thaw, and then you can type out his stories for me, and I'll add a few of my thoughts for a plot? Shouldn't take more than half an hour or so.' He turned towards the freezer.

Jade sighed. 'Okay.' She watched him for a second. 'You had a phone call while you were gone.'

'Oh?' Leaning into the freezer, Zan pawed through the packages. 'Who was it?'

'An old lover,' she said casually.

His hand stopped. Slowly, his shaggy head swung to face her. 'Is that a direct quote?' he asked quietly, his eyes scanning her face.

'It is.'

Gold brows twitched gently as his eyes lingered on her for a moment, then he turned back to the freezer. 'Oh.' He flipped carelessly through the packages. '. . . . What did she sound like?' he asked at last, his voice casual.

Jade searched for a diplomatic synonym for nasty. 'Crisp,' she hazarded, watching his profile.

The corner of his mouth shot up. 'Hmm,' he murmured noncommittally, pulling a package out and shutting the door. 'High voice? Low voice?' He turned to inspect her, his light eyes wary.

'Medium,' Jade smiled evilly. 'I couldn't tell if she had blue eyes or a wooden leg, from the conversation.'

The hard line of his lips quivered, then straightened again as he took her arm. He turned her towards the patio and gave a gentle shove. 'Man your typewriter, woman,' he commanded loftily, 'we still have work to do.'

The sun was setting as they finished. Jade leaned back in her director's chair to watch the show, while Zan stood behind her, leafing through the pages she'd typed. Wisps of cloud like pink flamingo feathers gleamed in the west. As she watched, they began to catch fire. Wherever she looked, the air glowed, bathing everything it touched in a golden haze. 'Look, Zan,' she breathed.

'I'm looking.' Warm and light, his hand fell on her shoulders.

They watched together in silence as the air shimmered. Finally, slowly, the light softened and cooled. Jade sighed happily. The gold was gone, flowing to the west in pursuit of the sun. But the water still gleamed pale silver, cupping the daylight even as the sky darkened above the town to the east. The gold hour was gone, the blue one just starting.

Jade sighed again. The warmth had gone with the sun and the heat of Zan's hand made the rest of her seem colder. She shivered and shrugged gently to break his grip, glancing up at him. 'That was the best sunset yet, Zan.'

Looking down at her, he nodded absently. 'Yes.' But his thoughts seemed far away. The hand on her shoulder tightened abruptly.

'Hadn't you better start the coals?' She pushed her chair back slowly, forcing him to move. It was time to break the spell.

'All right.' His hand dropped away, and she shivered again as the cool air found the spot he had abandoned. He remained standing, as if deep in thought, then turned towards the doorway. 'Come fix us a drink, while I do that.'

'All right.' That was a good sign. Zan rarely had a drink if he planned to work in the evening. Maybe she could get away early tonight and suddenly that seemed like a good idea. His quiet moods were the least predictable. Jade wondered if he would always make her nervous.

The phone rang as Jade entered the kitchen. She hesitated. Should she pick it up? It rang again.

'Will you get that, Jade?' Zan called from the patio.

Trust Zan to ignore the niceties, Jade thought wryly as she picked up the phone. His 'old lover' would hardly be overjoyed to know that she was still here. 'Hello?' she said briskly.

'*Oh*.' The throaty voice held a note of chilly surprise. 'It's you again. Put Zan on, please.'

Zan's big hand closed over the receiver as he loomed beside her. 'Thanks, Jade.' Holding the phone, he put his arm out as she tried to duck past him. 'Fix us those drinks, will you?' He pushed her gently down the counter towards the drinks cabinet, ignoring her frown, and put the phone to his ear. 'Hello?' he drawled.

Jade glared at the cabinets, her hands clenched. Zan had no decency at all! She didn't want to hear his romantic small talk! It was the *last* thing she cared to hear! And no doubt the woman on the other end of the line presumed Jade was out of earshot by now as well. She flicked a glance at him. How callous could he be?

Gold head cocked to hold the phone to his ear, Zan lounged back against the counter, one long leg casually stretched across the narrow kitchen and braced against the counter opposite, blocking her retreat. His long lips were tucked up at the corners in a faint smile as he listened.

She would make the drinks and escape, then. Jade swung open the cabinet and reached up for the gin.

'Yes,' Zan murmured into the phone, 'old lover—yes, she told me that.' He laughed softly. 'No, I'm afraid I didn't guess it was you, Irena. I've never thought of you as being that . . .' His voice trailed off delicately. 'How old *are* you?' he asked innocently.

Her hand on the tonic water, Jade froze, eyes widening. Had he really *said* that? She flicked a glance at him again. Zan's eyes were crinkled in silent laughter, but there was an ironic twist to his distant smile. His face looked harder than usual.

Jade set out the glasses and found the jigger, trying not to listen to Zan's seductive murmur.

'Mmm?' He paused. 'Yes, that's my secretary.' Jade

looked up to find his eyes on her. 'Yes, I felt in need of a new status symbol. Don't most successful authors have one?' The whimsical smile on his face could have been for Jade, or the woman on the phone, or perhaps both of them.

She looked down again to measure out the gin, her teeth slowly finding her lower lip.

'Yes, she does have a lovely voice, doesn't she?' Zan agreed smoothly.

This was getting a bit tiresome. Jade turned to frown her displeasure.

Zan measured her thoughtfully. 'Oh, I'd say about sixty to sixty-five,' he murmured, a laugh in his voice. 'Yes, I suppose she does sound younger. A very youthful sixty, then.' Anyone who knew him at all would recognise that note in his voice. He couldn't lie without it.

'Red,' he told the woman on the phone. 'Yes, that is a departure from my usual, isn't it? I suppose she dyes it to hide the grey.'

If the woman knew him at all, she wasn't buying this tale. And who was he teasing? The old love, Jade, or both of them? Jade splashed a chunk of ice in each glass and sliced the lime in one vicious, chopping stroke. She squeezed a slice into each glass, gave each drink a stir, and plunked one down by Zan. He winked in silent thanks.

Picking up her own drink, she smacked his knee briskly to make him move. She wanted out of here.

But Zan ignored the signal. His hard, gold-fuzzed leg stayed up, blocking the way. He stared absently into her angry eyes, then his smile deepened. 'Not much else,' he told his inquisitor. 'Big green eyes, jug ears, and an uncertain temper . . .' His cool eyes studied Jade's small, flushed ears mockingly.

That was enough. *Too* much. Jade set down her drink to make a determined assault on his leg. She didn't have to stay here and take this! Measuring his knee for the reflex point, she lifted her hand, but his leg dropped to the floor.

That was more like it. Picking up her drink again, she started to slide past him, her head high. But Zan's arm shot out to encircle her waist, and he hauled her in with a mischievous grin. 'Mmm-hmm,' he agreed to some comment.

This joke had gone too far! Eyes blazing, Jade clicked down her drink on the counter beside him. Bracing against his broad shoulders, she pushed back. But as the iron grip around her waist tightened, this simply arched her back over Zan's arm, bringing her breasts to his devilish attention. His pale eyes widened in a panto-mime of delighted lechery.

'No,' he was telling Irena. 'No, she's no distraction at all!' His head cocked to hold the phone, he grinned down teasingly into Jade's explosive face and gave her a friendly squeeze.

Jade clenched her teeth, fighting the impulse to smack him. The need to stay silent only increased her fury, and pushing was getting her nowhere. Beneath her out-spread fingers, Zan's heart beat with a rhythm that belied the smooth voice and the mischievous face. Slow-ly, she slid her hands across his chest and around to his sides. Could he be ticklish?

He studied her thoughtfully, his gold brows lifting warily. 'No,' he told his listener.

Jade fluttered her eyelashes to distract his attention as she searched for the most likely spots. As she found them, her eyes widened innocently just as her fingers jabbed into his ribs in sudden, vicious assault. Zan squirmed silently, eyes crinkling, then gasped as she found the right spot. His arm tightened in bruising response and Jade was suddenly crushed against him, his cast grinding into her stomach, her long legs tangling with his own. The rough, curly hair of his calves scratched electric shocks across her bare legs as her skirt rode up.

Rigid with outrage, Jade leaned back over his arm, glaring up at him, trying to minimise the contact as she panted for breath.

'Irena . . . yes, what were you . . . oh, yes, the work's going . . . very nicely.' Zan held her blazing gaze even as he continued the conversation. His grey eyes were darker now, the pupils dilated, and he wasn't smiling.

Breath regained, Jade made one last bone-cracking effort to free herself, twisting back against his arm in silent fury. The receiver dropped from his ear to fall clattering on the counter. Zan's arms slid up to her shoulders and he yanked her savagely up against him, crushing her breasts against his chest. His mouth caught her lips in a punishing, insolent kiss that took the last of her breath away.

'Hello? Zan? Hello?' The phone squawked beside them.

He was bending her slowly backwards, arching her breasts against him, his lips gentling from violence to a deliberate, devastating hunger. Even as her lips began to tremble and soften in answer, Zan tore his mouth away to stare down at her, his glittering eyes only inches from her own. '*Jade!*' he whispered. He bent his head again to brush her cheek with his lips, as his arm eased to let her down off her toes. Releasing her gently, he groped behind him for the telephone.

'Hello? *Hello!*' The voice was tiny and outraged.

Zan's eyes held her urgently even as he put the phone to his ear. 'Hello,' he said breathlessly. He took a deep breath, shaking the hair out of his eyebrows, his wide eyes still upon her. 'What's the problem, Irena, did you drop the phone?'

It took a second to realise she was free. Jade backed away a step, then whirled, breaking away from those compelling eyes. She stood still for a moment, knowing that she'd stumble if she tried to walk yet.

'Oh, well, it must be a bad connection,' Zan decided serenely behind her. He took another deep breath. 'Yes, we're on about the eighth chapter now.'

There was a long silence as he listened. 'No,' he finally said slowly. 'No, Irena, that's not such a good idea.' He sighed. 'You *would* be a distraction, and we can't have that, can we? You'd better wait a few weeks before visiting, okay?'

Jade straightened her shoulders with a small shudder. Now was the time to get out of here. She'd decide later if she was ever coming back. Her eyes filled with angry tears even as she looked around for her shoes.

'Mm-hmm,' Zan murmured. 'No, I don't think so.'

She glanced behind her, avoiding Zan's gaze. There were her shoes, of course, near the end counter by his big feet. Her jaw set in determination, she turned towards them.

'Irena,' Zan murmured urgently, 'I'm going to have to go now. I smell something burning.'

Jade put a hand on the sandals just as Zan's foot settled on top of them, anchoring them to the oak floor.

'Yes, I'm barbecuing, and it's definitely burning. 'Bye, love.' Zan jammed the phone down. 'Wait a minute, Jade.'

'Get off my shoes, damn you!' Jade wrenched one free and snatched for the other just as Zan stooped down to grab it. They straightened together, the sandal stretched shaking between them. 'Let *go*!' she raged.

Zan shook his head slowly, his cool gaze holding her stormy eyes. 'Not yet, Jade. Not till you let me say I'm sorry.' He took a deep breath.

'Oh, you're sorry all right,' she hissed up at him, her eyes swimming. 'You're the sorriest bastard I ever met!' She jerked the sandal again futilely and then, releasing it, smashed the other down next to his feet. '*Fine*, keep 'em as a souvenir!' She spun away towards the front door.

'Jade, *wait*!' Zan demanded.

She didn't bother to answer. To hell with him! She didn't even try to hurry as she stalked barefoot towards the exit. Let him try to stop her if he dared!

Zan's hand covered the doorknob just as she reached for it. Lifting her head proudly, she blasted him with one glittering look. He smiled crookedly and the door swung open before her. She swept out into the twilight and headed for home, the grass cold beneath her feet as the door shut softly behind her. *Damn* him! She took a deep breath and started up the road.

The gravel crunched beside her as a tall shape fell into step. 'Where are we going?' Zan asked mildly.

Jade didn't bother to turn her head. 'You can go to the devil, and I'm going home.' She shook her hair back and took another deep breath.

'Hmm.' He paced beside her, his long strides slow to match her clipped march.

It was dark under the trees as they climbed the hill away from the water. Except for his quiet breathing, she might have been alone. Jade pulled yet another deep breath of the night air, feeling her face begin to cool. The fine gravel of the drive bit into her feet, a half sensual, half painful sensation as the trembling began to leave her legs.

At the top of the hill, she paused, and felt him stop beside her. Turning, she looked back over the harbour. Anchor lights bobbed on a few yachts here and there, and the round yellow lights were their portholes, lit from within. The green light of a channel buoy flashed its monotonous, soothing message to the night, and beyond all this, the bridge crowned the black sky.

Zan knelt before her suddenly, his hand encircling her ankle.

It was a struggle to keep her voice level. 'Let go of me, Zan,' she breathed dangerously.

His low voice was carefully neutral. 'You're going to hurt your feet, Jade, if you don't wear shoes.' Lifting her foot, he set it on his thigh where he could reach it with both hands, and began to strap her sandal on. The firmness of his grip warned her not to resist.

It was strangely stirring, feeling Zan's warm, hesitant fingers play across her skin in the dark. The crisp hair of his thigh scratched electric, quivering telegrams into the flinching sole of her captive foot. And as he worked with slow, intense deliberation, his thick hair brushing her bare leg, goosebumps spread up her thighs and changed to a sensation of heat.

Zan's hand squeezed her ankle gently as he finished the right foot. He set it down and reached for the other. He turned her foot gently to get at the buckle and she swayed as she lost her balance. There was nothing to grab hold of but Zan. She caught herself against his wide shoulders, felt the muscles tense as his fingers stopped on her foot. After a second, his hands moved again, gentle, clumsy, soothing. Through her palms, she could feel the pulse in his neck—a deeper, stronger echo of her own heart's pumping.

Zan tugged the last strap into place, and then his hand closed on her ankle again, his fingers wrapping right around it. As she stirred, his head turned quickly, his hair brushing her calf. Warm and electric, his mouth found the inside of her knee. His lips were slightly parted, his breath steaming across her skin, firing it, sending hot tremors surging up her thigh and across her loins.

Gasping, Jade pulled back, her eyes filling with tears, and he let her go. Her legs were shaking again as he stood to look down at her, and suddenly she wished she could see his eyes. What would she see there right now? She turned away, walking slowly now, and after a long moment, Zan moved beside her again, a sombre, silent shadow. A man she didn't know at all. Had never really known.

The lush, overgrown landscaping of the cove area gave way to the close-set houses of the town as they neared her neighbourhood. Jade could see him in the occasional street light now as he padded beside her, shaggy head bent in thought, good hand in the pocket of his shorts. As a car passed them Zan looked up and met her eyes for an instant. He smiled crookedly and looked down again, his brows knotted.

'Zan?' She hadn't meant to speak, but suddenly the words were there.

'Hmm?' His head leaned a little closer, but he kept his eyes on their path.

'Why did you make me listen to that phone call?' Suddenly it seemed very important to know. Had there been any reason at all, other than mischief?

'I wanted . . .' Zan's low voice trailed away into silence. He walked on, head bent, oblivious to her sidelong glance. His thick brows lifted and dropped in a small shrug. 'I don't know, Jade.' He shot a glance at her. 'I don't know . . .'

Jade studied his hard, clear profile for a second and sighed. For no reason at all, then. It figured. Just Zan's brand of innocent fun.

'—but you know I didn't mean to hurt you!' He caught her arm suddenly and swung her to face him. 'You do know that, don't you, Jade?' he demanded, his pale eyes searching her face, his eyebrows a remorseful, shaggy line. She flinched as his fingers tightened unconsciously.

'Yes, Zan, I know that.' She sighed again, looking down, and after a second he released her. Turning, Jade walked on, her eyes on the sidewalk. And it was the truth. Zan would never hurt her intentionally, any more than he would hurt his Irena, or his Mona, or any other woman unfortunate enough to love him. He was as innocent, and as heartless, as a young lion playing with a rabbit. And like the lion, she guessed that Zan knew nothing of pain nor heartache. But the rabbit learns soon enough. She looked up. They were nearly at her corner. 'This is where I turn off.'

'Don't go yet. Let's walk into town, find some seafood.'

She shook her head. 'Not tonight, Zan.'

His thick brows pulled into a small frown, Zan stared down at her silently, assessing her resistance. Finally his chest lifted in a slow sigh. 'You know, I get lonesome too,' he remarked humbly. 'Couldn't we be lonesome together? I'd behave myself.'

'You'd behave yourself according to my terms or according to yours, Zan?' she asked carefully.

His grey eyes widened. 'Yours, sweet, if I can figure what they are,' he said softly. 'If I step over the line tonight, just tell me, okay?'

Jade studied him sceptically. There was a catch somewhere, she knew. With Zan there was always a catch. 'You promise?'

'I promise.' Eyes gleaming, he offered his good hand to close the deal.

He was impossible—and irresistible. Shrugging ruefully, she gave him her hand.

Solemnly, awkwardly Zan shook it, then turned towards town, still holding on to her. 'So where do we find a lobster in this burg?' he asked over his shoulder, pulling her along gently.

Jade bit her lip. He just didn't quit, did he? She gave a gentle tug, and scowled when he ignored it. 'Zan . . .' she growled ominously. She had no intention of walking in to town hand in hand with the brute.

'Hmm, sweet?' Still walking, he glanced down at her, eyes wide and innocent.

'You're over the line already,' she told him.

'Line? . . . Oh, you mean *this*?' He lifted her hand to

study it as they walked. 'I'm supposed to give it back now?' His lips curled in spite of his efforts to look indignant.

'That's the custom,' she said dryly.

He squeezed it gently and released her, then took a deep breath. 'Guess I was thinking of some other custom, sweet,' he said quietly. 'Sorry.'

When they reached the waterfront, Zan took her hand again and towed her behind him, breasting the stream of pedestrians like a big tug. Jade followed docilely in his wake, eyeing the jammed sidewalks with dismay. The tourists were out en masse tonight, blue-blazered yachtsmen crammed shoulder to shoulder with kids in tee-shirts and skin-tight jeans. A bare-chested fisherman in cut-offs and seaboots bounced off Zan's chest and staggered past, cutting in front of a pair of blue-haired matrons in mink and diamonds. Bright colours and bare skin flowed around them in a dizzying splendour punctuated by blocks of dazzling white, as Navy officers from the War College up the bay steamed past in close-ranked convoy. Ahead of her, Zan was losing way as he craned to take all this in and navigate as well. Reaching the eddy of a street light post, he swung into it and pulled her to him, his arm wrapping around her to hold her against the current. 'My God, if it's like this on a Thursday, what's it like on a weekend?' he marvelled, his mouth at her ear.

'This is Saturday, you hermit!' she laughed up at him. 'This is *the* scene. Half the state comes here to strut their stuff!'

'Saturday?' His gold brows twitched gently as his head swung to follow the passage of three girls in bikini tops and flowing cotton skirts. He turned back to her, smiling. 'Okay, it's Saturday, if you say so. Where do we eat?' His hand tightened around her shoulders and he pulled her against his chest as two kids careened by on roller skates.

'Without a reservation?' Jade frowned against his

neck, the gold hairs in the open vee of his shirt drawing her eyes. 'How about a clam shack?'

But Zan shook his head, his chin grazing her hair. 'Something nicer, Jade. Show me a good restaurant—I hear the town's full of 'em.'

'Okay,' she agreed doubtfully. 'I suppose we can try. My favourite's on this next wharf, down near the water. Take a left after that art gallery.'

'Right.' Zan pushed out into the stream, to forge a slow and steady passage across the mob's flow with Jade huddled behind his wide shoulders, her hand held fast and safe in his casual paw.

Galleries, shops and bars lined the cobblestoned alley leading down to the docks. Edging their way through the swirling throng outside an outdoor bar, they turned another corner, leaving the cheerful din of the bar scene for the sound of the sea lapping against the pilings and the wind-chime tapping of a loose halyard against an aluminium mast.

'Ah,' Zan breathed, 'this is more like it! Is that your restaurant?' He nodded towards the low, shingled building that extended out over the water, its windows flickering with candlelight and moving shapes beyond.

'Mm-hm. But it looks pretty crowded.' Jade stopped in front of a boutique across from the entrance. They were wasting their time. Although it was not a part of the frantic social scene just around the corner, this restaurant had a solid reputation with the locals and yachtsmen who sailed up to its docks for an evening of seafood and quiet music. It would be full.

'Well, we'll see what we can do,' Zan smiled. 'Want to wait here?'

'All right.' She watched him pad away across the cobblestones, then turned to the shop windows at her back. Focussing on a blue-green bikini, her favourite shade, she tried to blot out the image of his long-legged casual stride, the feel of his hand.

In a few minutes, Zan was back, two drinks clutched in one hand and looking quite pleased with himself. Touching her shoulder, he turned to saunter out along the dock past the restaurant. 'Let's look at some boats,' he suggested, beginning to smile.

'And supper?' she asked, her stomach seconding the question with a soft growl.

'They'll take us, but we've an hour to kill yet.'

Boards echoing hollowly under their slow feet, they moved in companionable silence, stopping to admire each boat as they came to it. Zan finished his drink and balanced the glass carefully on the dock's railing. His head turned towards Jade. Still walking, she ignored his scrutiny, her eyes flicking nervously to the boats ahead of them.

Finally Zan spoke. 'You know, Jade, for someone with . . . auburn hair, you're surprisingly non-violent,' he remarked quietly.

'How's that?' she asked over her shoulder as she walked on, the thin cotton of her dress billowing back against her legs with the breeze off the water, her hair fluttering off her shoulders in slow, silky waves.

'Well, I would have thought that in our . . . difference this evening a slap might have been the accepted female response,' Zan said thoughtfully. 'And though you look rather fragile, I suspect you pack a pretty good wallop, so why the scruples? Is it against your principles as a liberated female?'

Jade shook her head, frowning down as their toes hit the dock in perfect step. 'No,' she said lightly, 'it isn't. But the one time I ever tried it, I picked on a liberated male.' Suddenly she was cold. She hugged herself, rubbing her bare arms as they roughened in the breeze.

'And?' Zan asked quietly, bumping against her shoulder.

'And nothing,' she said quickly, wishing she'd never spoken. She began to walk faster.

'And . . . what . . . happened?' he repeated beside her, giving each word a weight which emphasised his sudden determination to know.

Jade sighed in exasperation. 'And he nearly knocked me cold,' she said flatly.

Zan's fingers bit into her arm as he swung her to face him. His face was hard and frozen, only the bruising pressure of his fingers giving a clue to his temper. 'Zan!'

'Who?' he bit out carefully. 'Lover boy?' His eyes caught the lights from the shore, and threw them back glittering.

Suddenly she was as angry as he was. Why couldn't he mind his own business? She jerked her arm, but his grip held—loosened a little, but held. 'No, not Fred. Would you let me go, please?'

'Who, then, and when, please?' Zan demanded coldly, his icy eyes scanning her face as he ignored the request.

Jade took a deep, steadying breath, her green eyes wide and determined. 'Look, I'm sorry I mentioned it, but I really don't want to talk about it, Zan.' She jerked her arm again, but it might as well have been cast in concrete.

He pulled her closer. 'Just tell me—'

'Zan,' she cut in passionately, 'correct me if I'm wrong, but I thought you'd already apologised once tonight for manhandling me.' She slanted a bitter glance at the hand clamped around her arm and then stared up into the hard face above her. 'Do I get another apology once this is over?'

Zan's eyes shifted to his hand, and then back to her face as his grip eased. He sighed impatiently, his fingers tracing her bare arm down to the elbow in an absent caress before dropping away. 'Why—'

'Zan, I don't want to fight, and I *don't* want to talk about it. Lay off!' She shook the hair back from her cheeks and frowned up at him, willing him not to spoil this evening.

A muscle jumped along his jaw. 'Okay—okay, okay, *okay*!' he muttered savagely, wheeling away from her. He stalked further out the dock, and, reaching the end of it, slouched against a piling to stare out into the dark harbour, his broad shoulders strained tight.

Jade stayed where she was, shivering. She turned to stare blindly at the boat tied below her in the water, trying not to think . . . How had Zan got that out of her? She didn't let herself *think* about Jack, much less discuss him. Since that night, she'd packed him away, walled him off into a corner of her mind, shutting the pain and the humiliation out of her consciousness.

But Zan had pulled a brick out of that wall tonight, and as the minutes passed and her mind waited, wincing, it was rather stunning to find that no pain blew through the gap. Where and when had it gone? And what was left? All she could find at the moment was a wry incredulity. How could she have ever fallen for such a man in the first place? And how long had she been free of him, without even knowing it?

A long arm wrapped around her shoulders. 'You're freezing, aren't you, sweet? Let's get out of this wind.' Zan pulled her gently towards the shore, his face sombre and preoccupied. He glanced down at her as they left the dock, and his eyes narrowed. 'And who is that funny little smile for, Red?' he asked roughly.

Jade shook her head, tried to swallow it, and failed. This one was for Zan, but she couldn't tell him that, could she?

With half an hour left to kill, they wandered the wharves. By unspoken agreement, they avoided the mixers in front of the bars in favour of window-shopping. Fine silver, hand-made pottery, nautical knick-knacks, high fashion—all these and more could be found in the tasteful and expensive shops they

strolled past. They browsed through a bookstore, and
Jade went directly to the thriller section. Eagerly she
checked the shelves—Haggerty, Hailey . . . Halloran.
She blinked. There were more than she had expected.
This last week or so, she had come to think of writing as
being an agonisingly slow, often frustrating process. But
judging from the number of titles here, apparently Zan
did not always write so slowly—if this work was indeed
Zan's. Jade pulled one out at random, made a face at the
cover, and flipped it open to read the front copy. And
reading, she began to smile. So he *was* Wyk Halloran—it
hadn't been a joke. His style was unmistakable. She
found the one she wanted and made Zan loan her the
money to buy it, in spite of his mocking disgust.

'Why not?' he shrugged finally. 'You've got everything else.' He jerked his chin towards the door. 'Come
on, Jade, we've got to go. I worked hard for that
reservation.'

At the restaurant, the blonde hostess greeted Zan like
a long-lost and very dear friend. Jade found that Zan's
hard work had earned them a table for two next to the
windows—the choicest location. The hostess led them to
it, swaying beside Zan as they walked, her generous,
earthy curves bumping softly against him twice as they
skirted the tables.

Zan seated Jade with careful, clumsy courtesy, and an
appreciative word to the blonde. As she gave him the
menus, her breast brushed his shoulder in the lightest of
touches. And then she was slinking away again, her long
gown whispering. Not once had she even glanced at
Jade.

Speechless, Jade looked up from the candle on the
table between them. Menus in hand, Zan sat frozen, his
eyes wide and darkened with the flare of his black pupils,
his face a study in granite. The thick lashes swept down
in a slow blink and he glanced up at her, and then quickly
away again, but not before she had seen the anger and

the arousal in his wide eyes. A pain like a thread of fire whipped around her heart and pulled tight. Was this what Irena had felt when she answered the phone?

'Nice place,' Zan commented huskily. His lips twisted up in a slight, rueful grin as he heard his own voice and he turned back to her, the hard look slowly fading to an apologetic smile. 'I hear they even serve food here,' he remarked wryly, handing her a menu.

Although she knew what she would have already, Jade took it and studied it intently, hiding behind her long lashes. When had Zan last had a woman, she wondered, that he should look so hungry just then? How long *had* Mona been gone? She bit her lip thoughtfully. For that matter, why conclude that Mona was the last woman he'd taken to bed? Demonstrably, all Zan had to do was whistle. No wonder she frustrated him sometimes!

Her hands clenched as the thought hit home; had Zan ever found a woman he couldn't have, before? Was that why she seemed to intrigue him sometimes? Zan liked a challenge as well as the next man—probably preferred it to having his conquests handed him on a platter, judging from the anger in his face a moment ago. The thought was particularly depressing. She did *not* want to be an abstract challenge to Zan, an object to be reached and mastered.

'Well, Jade?' She'd been so far away, it was a shock to find Zan sitting there before her. His gold brows knotted as he searched her face, his grey eyes puzzled. 'What'll you have?'

She had to pull herself together. 'Are you feeling rich, Zan?' she asked lightly.

'Rich enough. And this is a celebration. What'll it be?'

'The stuffed lobster, please. What are we celebrating?' Or should she have asked that?

But he shook his head slowly, his eyes holding hers.

'I'm not sure yet,' he said softly. 'Isn't it National Grape Stompers Week?'

Jade raised an eyebrow. 'Then what was last week?'

'American Mud-Volleyball Week,' he said gravely.

Smiling, she pulled her eyes away to study the harbour beyond the glass. A late moon must have risen. She couldn't see it from here, but its moonbeams skittered over the water like pearls bouncing across a black mirror. The dark shapes of the boats curtsied and bowed at their moorings in the dancing light.

While Zan ordered, Jade pulled his book out of the bag. She thumbed slowly through the opening pages and came to the dedication. 'To Al and to Mona', it said. She shut the book again quickly, to find him watching her. 'Who's Al?' she asked breathlessly.

'He's the rookie cop I lived with day and night for nearly a year to get that story.'

She flipped on restlessly through the pages. 'And did this book do well?'

Zan smiled ruefully. 'I made almost enough to pay my father back for the year's tuition at Columbia I'd thrown away.'

'You failed college?' she asked incredulously. It was hard to imagine a college course that could faze him.

'I dropped out too late to withdraw honourably, my junior year.' His lips quirked at some memory. 'Mona was there, getting a business degree, at the time. She persuaded me that if I was serious about writing, it was time to dump the English courses and put up or shut up. She was right, of course—she always is.' The warm smile now lighting his face was not for Jade, but slowly his eyes came back to her. 'That's why this book is for her, as well.'

'So this is your first book,' Jade concluded absently, her thoughts on the woman who had made it possible. Mona again . . . So he'd known her that long. The pattern was clear. There were other experiences, other women, other facets of his life, but in the end, Zan came back to Mona. He probably always would.

When the food and the wine came, Zan set himself to entertain. While Jade cracked his boiled lobster for him, he told her about the year in New York as a city cop's shadow and alter ego. It was a carefully edited version, she suspected, all gloom and gore deleted, the strange and the good times shamelessly embroidered. She laughed until the couple at the next table stared and Zan hushed her, only to tell stories even more outrageously in whisper and pantomime.

When the plates had been cleared and the coffee brought round at last, Zan grew quiet, slowly drawing into himself to stare down at the cup before him. Jade didn't mind the silence, she was used to watching him think by now. He was probably writing in his head at the moment, and she only hoped it would keep until tomorrow. She was in no mood to type tonight—too happy, too peaceful for that.

Jade took another sip of coffee and leaned back in her chair, her eyes on his big-boned wrist, the long fingers curled absently around his cup. And in the unguarded moment, the thought eased gently and inevitably into her mind—or rather, words came at last to fit the wordless instincts she'd been fighting for weeks; what kind of lover would Zan be? Her heart accelerated with the question as she studied that hand. She thought she knew now. He'd be the same, only more so. He'd be gentle and lunatic, friend and tyrant, unbelievably strong and never quite predictable. He'd be heart-breakingly tender with her body while he demolished her heart, and finally—he'd be gone.

'I believe it's illegal to look like that in a public restaurant, Jade. What are you thinking just now?'

Fantasy meshed with reality as their eyes met and the blood leaped to her face. Zan was real, he was here, and for a second, Jade wasn't sure into which world she was waking—only that he was there with her, and that she stood naked before him, defenceless before his wide-eyed, probing scrutiny.

Wrenching her eyes away, Jade broke the contact to stare across the restaurant, feeling the fire in her cheeks, the heat of his eyes scorching her profile. 'I was . . . just thinking of the last time I ate here,' she lied breathlessly. She found she was staring at the hostess, as the woman swivelled across the room to greet an incoming couple, and she transferred her gaze to the candle before her.

But Zan was not satisfied yet. 'And when was that?' he pressed sceptically, his voice warmly taunting.

When . . . she searched for the answer, numb with embarrassment, and found it with an inward jolt that brought her eyes up to meet his dancing gaze. How could she have forgotten that? 'The night Fred and I became engaged,' she blurted.

His chin jerked slightly as his head came up, the laughter freezing in his eyes. His face closed. 'Oh,' he said flatly.

Jade looked down at her clenched hands, suddenly miserable. The fragile bond that had tied them together tonight was snapped, broken by her own clumsy words. She was sitting with a stranger. Suddenly she had to get away. 'If you'll excuse me a moment, Zan . . .' He nodded silently, looking past her shoulder, his mouth a straight line as she fled.

Fool! she told the pale face that stared back at her from the mirror in the women's room. *You fool, didn't you learn the last time?* But she knew now that that last heartache hadn't prepared her for Zan's explosive potential, any more than a head cold prepares one for a bout of bubonic plague. It had taken her a year to get over Jack's shabby little con game. How long would it take to recover from Zan, if she were to fall in love with

him? Zan, who would take and give without apology or
deception . . .

If . . . Her eyes in the glass before her were huge.
They looked almost black, the pupils dilated and puls-
ing. You're not that stupid, she told herself. You've
been through the fire once, and now you've found a good
man. A long-term man. Don't throw him away for a
lighthearted, light-loving joker like Zan! What do you
want? A summer of 'fun' as he put it, or a lifetime of
kindness and caring? Make your choice! She took a deep
breath, and began to smooth her windblown hair. No,
she wasn't such a fool . . . Her mother might be, but she
was not.

And neither was the hostess, Jade decided when she
finally returned to the dining room. The blonde stood at
their table, one hip cocked, her red-tipped fingers resting on the edge of the table by Zan's arm as she smiled
down at him. Bright head uplifted, Zan returned the
smile with a mocking, lazy look that Jade had never seen
before.

She stopped in the doorway, feeling like a fool—an
intruding fool at that. And she'd actually worried about
Zan's needs as well as her own! A shimmer of undirected
rage swept through her. She was an idiot! Zan could take
very good care of himself, thank you. Perhaps she
should go back to the women's room, or perhaps even
home, and leave him to make his contact, to fill those
needs, since she had nothing to give him.

Across the room, Zan's eyes dropped from the
woman, swung around to pin her in the doorway as his
smile faded. His brows twitched gently—a silent message that she couldn't interpret. His eyes still holding her,
he answered the woman absently, and she laughed and
glided away, a satisfied smirk on her handsome face.
And Zan simply waited, his cool eyes holding her,
studying her with detached and sombre interest as she
approached.

'I ordered you a liqueur.' He nodded to the glass before her.

'Thank you, but I didn't want one,' she told him as she sat down.

'So drink it anyway.' He swirled his glass in the candlelight between them, watching the pale liquid revolve and gleam.

'Yes, Master,' she murmured insolently, taking a sip as she met those glittering eyes. The brandy burned her tongue, exploded softly in the back of her mouth, and blazed a warm, vaporous comet trail down her throat. She took another sip. 'Get yourself a date?' she asked mockingly, her eyes flicking towards his friend across the room.

Zan didn't pretend to misunderstand her as his head lifted dangerously. His mouth hardened. 'I don't "date" when I'm writing, Jade. It's too distracting,' he said evenly.

'Oh?' The word came out sounding more challenging than she'd meant it to be.

'Neither do I fight with people I like. Nor do I waste time going out to supper in the middle of a book like this.' He tipped his glass and finished the last of the brandy.

Jade widened her eyes. 'Oh?' It was a stupid syllable, but it seemed to annoy him, and that more than justified its use at the moment.

'Yes, "oh", Red,' he mimicked savagely. 'This is a first for me, but don't let it bother you. It's just another of my rules I've had to break since you barged into my life.' Reaching across the table, he plucked the glass out of her startled fingers. He twirled it slowly, until finding the place her lips had touched, he drained the glass, his eyes taunting her as he drank. 'Since you didn't want it . . .' he explained mockingly. Rubbing the edge of the glass against his lips, he studied her flushed face. 'And in case you hadn't noticed, the book's not going so well either,' he finished ironically, holding the empty glass out to her.

Jade ignored it. 'What you're saying is that I'm bothering you.'

'Bright girl!' he applauded, setting the glass before her with insolent precision.

She took a deep breath. There must be some way to hurt him as well. She smiled. 'Well, that's easily solved, isn't it?' she said lightly. 'I've sold eight paintings and my car this month—I'm rich. Let me buy you a dictaphone, and I'll buy me a ticket to Greece, where I'm still wanted.'

Zan's head lifted slowly. 'Mention Greece again and I'll break your neck,' he drawled politely, his voice at its gentlest. 'You made a promise, if you'll recall.'

It was as good an exit line as she would find. 'Promises can be broken,' she remarked sweetly, starting to rise.

He had her wrist before she could straighten, as a glass smashed over with a soft tinkle. 'Sit . . . down,' he breathed, his eyes blazing with cold fire.

Jade sat, feeling rather than seeing the faces at the next table turn their way. She shut her eyes as the tears started to gather. Blood pounded in her captive wrist, but whether it was Zan's pulse or her own, she couldn't tell. She took a shaking breath. How had this started? How could an evening move from laughter to anger to tears in the space of a few words?

For a long moment, they were both still, perhaps both sharing the same strange feeling of déjà vu. Finally Zan lifted her hand and rubbed it slowly across his lips, his hard cheek. 'God! What are you trying to prove?' he whispered against her skin.

'You need a shave,' she pointed out, her eyes still closed, as she tried to fight the tears and the sweet, languid sensations coursing up her arm.

'That's not what I need.' He spoke the words into the palm of her hand, his breath steaming against her flesh.

'Shall I tell you what I need, Jade?' His tongue traced the soft web between her thumb and forefinger. 'I'll say it right here,' he told her, 'but grab it quick. It's a secret, and I don't want those snoops at the next table to know.'

Jade shook her head, trying to close her fingers against his secret as her eyes shut him out, but he pressed her palm against his lips, forcing it open, his teeth bruising the soft skin.

'Zan—'

'Ask me what I need,' he insisted, his mouth moving against her hand.

'Zan!'

'It's okay, sweet, I've got all night,' he reassured her, his words tickling and warm. 'I'll wait.'

She sighed, defeated. 'What do you need?'

'You,' he said huskily, dropping it into her palm with a kiss. His hand slid up to close her fingers over it. 'You can open your eyes now,' he told her gently. 'And yes, I'm sorry. How many apologies does that make tonight?'

'I've lost count,' she said bitterly, turning to stare out the window, her hand clenched tightly under the table.

They walked back in silence, their steps measured and slow in the late night stillness, their shadows black and small as the three-quarter moon rode high. Only when he guided her up the front steps did it dawn on Jade that, as far as Zan knew, she still lived on the second floor, and she winced at the thought of his discovering her deception. Not tonight! There had been enough hurts traded back and forth already, tonight.

At the front door, she turned to lean back against it, smiling up at him. 'Well, Zan, thanks for supper,' she said briskly, willing him to leave now.

His brows twitched gently as he scanned her face. 'My pleasure,' he said finally, his hand closing on the doorknob beside her. Obviously he intended to see her up the stairs.

If she stood here much longer, he'd think she was waiting for a kiss, she realised. 'Goodnight,' she told him firmly, holding her ground.

But Zan shook his head. 'Not till I check your stairs for cat burglars and assorted crazies, it isn't, Jade. Move,' he ordered.

She stepped aside, hissing in exasperation. Let him look, then, since she couldn't stop him! But her eyes fell on the mailbox, and the solution to her problem. Snatching the blue airmail letter out of the box, she stepped lightly back across the porch to perch on the top step. Good old Fred. He always came through when she needed him, didn't he?

'What do you think you're doing, Jade?' Looking back from the doorway, Zan sounded thoroughly out of temper.

'My letter from Fred finally came,' she explained. 'The mail's unbelievably slow from there!' She made as if to open it.

'That's nice,' Zan said evenly. 'Bring it along and you can open it in a minute.'

Jade shook her head gaily. 'There's moon enough to read by. It's more romantic out here.' She looked up at him pleadingly. 'Please go home, Zan. You're tired. I'll go up in a minute.' She stroked the letter nervously.

Cursing softly, he threw himself down beside her. The top step squealed. 'Fine! Be difficult. Go ahead and read it,' he bit out savagely. He tossed the book he'd been carrying for her into her lap. Leaning back against the porch railing, he glared at her and rubbed the back of his neck.

Her temper flaring to match his own, Jade could almost believe the letter was the real issue. Chin tilted defiantly, she shook her hair back and scowled up at him. 'Zan, this is a personal, private, *special* letter,' she enunciated carefully. 'Do I have to spell it out for you? Go home!'

He lunged forward as if to grab hold of her, but caught his balance on the step beside her instead. 'Want me to spell out what happens to little girls who sit out on the street at one in the morning, with their eyes on their letters and their minds in Greece?' he snarled into her face. 'We read about 'em in the paper the next day, and it's not in the comic section! You go upstairs and I'll gladly go home.'

Jade took a deep breath and held it, staring up into his blazing eyes. His breath warmed her face, he was so near. It would be so easy to touch his cheek, turn that rage to—'Zan,' she said softly, 'this isn't New York City, I'm not a little girl, and I go to bed when and where I choose. Is that clear?'

'Quite!' He was off the steps and on to his feet in one surge, stood towering above her. Glaring down at her, he breathed deeply, started to speak, then wheeled away instead and padded off.

'Zan!' She couldn't let him go like that. 'Zan, *please*!'

He spun around, a tall, indistinct shape in the moonlight, head high and waiting.

'I . . . please . . .' She had nothing planned to say. Nothing she *could* say. 'What time do you want me there tomorrow?'

'I *don't* want you tomorrow.'

It was a crisp, free-swinging verbal backhand, and tears stung her eyes as it landed. 'Oh . . . when—'

'I'll call you.' Zan backed away a step, his mind already gone from here. 'I need a few days to think.' He turned away again.

Anger flooded in to fill the hollow space in her stomach. 'I may not be near a phone these next few days!' she called after him defiantly.

'You'd *better* be!' The words floated back over his

shoulder and then he was gone, a long-legged, tear-blurred shadow fading into the moonlight.

Jade sat on the steps a long time, the letter forgotten in her lap. Finally, wiping her eyes, she crept around to the back door to let herself in.

CHAPTER SEVEN

ROLLING off of her stomach and out of a dream, Jade groped for the phone by the mattress and lifted it on the second ring. She flopped back against the pillow, with the receiver at her ear and her eyes closed.

'Red?' Zan's voice tickled her ear, sending an unconscious smile spreading across her face.

Her eyes fluttered open and she grinned up at the newly painted ceiling. She'd painted walls, trim, and ceiling all day yesterday, finished long after midnight. It looked lovely. And the light coming in the kitchen window through the herbs promised a lovely day. She sighed softly. Lovely.

'Anybody there?' he murmured curiously.

His words sent a slow shiver rippling across her bare body beneath the sheet. She gripped the receiver harder and tried to wake up. 'Nobody here by that name,' she breathed at last.

'Hmm.'

Jade closed her eyes and pictured him leaning back against the counter, the gold hair falling down towards his shaggy brows, a faint smile tugging at his long lips.

'Well have you seen anyone around there with green eyes and auburn hair, who types and cracks eggs?'

Still smiling, Jade brushed a lock of hair out of her eyes. 'I could check, sir. Do you have any messages if I find such a person?'

'Yes, would you tell her that after three days of cold cereal my spirit is well and truly broken? And that I'll take her and her omelettes back on any terms she'll give me?'

'*Any* terms?' Jade purred, stretching luxuriously.

'Umm . . . Well, let me rephrase that,' Zan murmured thoughtfully. 'Tell her if she doesn't get her little self over here pronto there's going to be hell to pay. You spell that B-i-g T-r-o-u-b-l-e, comma, R-e-d. Hell . . . to . . . pay. Got that, sweetheart?'

'Yes, sir, I will relay that message, sir. Is there anything else?' She sat up slowly.

'Yes,' the low voice had roughened and dropped even lower, 'tell her—'

'Yes?' A prickle of uneasiness shook her shoulders.

There was an instant of silence and then she heard him exhale slowly. 'Forget it,' he said briskly. 'Don't be long.' The phone clicked in her ear.

Thoughtfully, Jade put down the phone and stared at it. After a moment she found she was grinning again. She shook her head briskly and stood up, wandered smiling to the bathroom to find her hairbrush. So he had forgiven her after all. Or rather, decided he needed her. For a while there, she'd wondered if he would. She'd spent the last three days in a restless limbo – painting the kitchen, cursing the plants, waiting . . .

Absently, she set the unused brush on the kitchen counter, and pinning her hair back, washed her face in the kitchen sink. The one in the bathroom was hopelessly clogged.

Zan would know how to unclog a sink . . . Pity she couldn't ask his advice. Ah well, she shrugged and grinned at the plants. She'd just have to fix it herself. This morning she felt as if she could fix anything.

Humming, Jade brushed her hair out until it crackled. She swung right side up again and continued brushing, and found she was facing Fred's photograph at the end of the counter. Slowly, her smile faded. It wasn't fair. How could she miss Zan more in three days than she'd missed Fred in a month? How could she?

'Fred . . .' she appealed to the picture, and stopped,

biting her lip. What could she ask of him, after all? Patience? He was giving her that already. His letter had been more than patient—as well as confused, hurt and exasperated. Where had she been the two times he'd made it into town to call her? What was going on? . . . What was this mysterious debt she'd incurred? . . . Did she still love him? . . . *Well?* She shook her head angrily. 'It's not fair, Fred, . . . or maybe I'm not.' For it was her fault. Somehow. She couldn't really blame Zan. He hadn't asked to be run down, after all. It must be her fault.

And she was going to be late. Big trouble and hell to pay, with a hungry man waiting . . . Two men waiting . . . She spun away, picked out a blouse of blue gauze that he'd never seen before, and dressed quickly. She was smiling again by the time she bounced out of the back door. She glanced around jubilantly—blue sky, early morning sunshine, mocking-bird singing in the next yard—lovely day!

But no one answered her jaunty rap on Zan's door when she arrived, and her smile faded. Somehow she had expected Zan to throw open the door at her first knock. Where was he? She tried again with the same result, considered the door bell and decided not to ring. Shrugging wryly, she fished her key ring out of her pocket. He had forced a key on her a few weeks, back, although she had never had to use it before. 'Zan?' she called as she stepped inside.

Nothing. She walked into the room, remembering her fear the first time she had entered it. Now it was like coming home again. 'Zan?'

No answer. The glass doors to the patio were open though, the leaves of her begonia lifting in the soft breeze. She walked outside. Not on the patio, but at the end of the dock . . . Jade stared. A small, neat sailboat was tied off, facing the harbour. Something moved in its cockpit, a dark blond, tousselled cap of hair. Zan.

Jade crept down the dock, her eyes fixed on the back of his head. Long legs stretched out on the seat before him, Zan lounged back in the deep cockpit, his head resting against the back edge of the deck. As he moved suddenly, lifting a cup of coffee to drink, Jade froze, admiring the hard line of his high cheekbone broken by the soft blur of his lashes. He turned towards her, jerked in alarm and the coffee sloshed over.

'Son of a—' he gasped, and set the cup down, shaking his hand and scowling up at her. 'You'll kill me yet, Jade! Motorised assault, heart attack, or scalding—One way or another, you'll get me in the end!'

Laughing in spite of herself, she came forward. 'I'm sorry, Zan, are you okay?' She sat down on the edge of the sailboat. It rocked gently, then steadied again.

'Yes,' he growled, sucking his fingers, 'I'm fine.' His eyes raked slowly across her face as his sunbleached eyebrows relaxed. 'That was quick,' he added absently. 'I didn't expect you for half an hour or so.'

'From the message I got, I figured I'd better hurry!' She tore her eyes away from his face to inspect the boat. 'This is some yacht,' she teased. 'Can I come aboard?'

'I believe you are already. Shows a distinct lack of nautical etiquette,' he grumped, leaning over to inspect her feet. 'Rule number one is no street shoes aboard. Off with those sandals!'

Grinning, Jade obeyed, kicking them off on the dock. Nothing had changed, and she had to swallow a laugh of pure joy. Lifting her long legs, she pivotted around to swing them into the cockpit, which was shaped like an oversized bathtub, with a bench running fore and aft along each side of it. 'Where did you get this?' she asked happily.

Zan looked up from her legs, his eyes gleaming. 'Chartered it for a month,' he said absently. 'Now come sit down and tell me what you know about sailing.'

'Port, starboard, mast, boom, hard alee and avast,'

Jade rattled off smugly as she settled down on the bench opposite him. 'Oh, and mayday, mayday, mayday—period.'

Zan made a face. 'I was afraid of that. Okay, we'll start with vocabulary.'

'After coffee,' Jade pleaded, spotting the coffee pot placed on the after deck.

'Mind using my cup?' Zan collected it off the floor-boards and looked up at her, shaking the loose hair out of his eyebrows. 'It's the only one here.'

She shook her head slowly, smiling, then looked away again quickly as she felt her colour rise. After a moment, she felt his eyes leave her face as he poured out the coffee. 'What's its name?' she asked breathlessly.

'Her name,' he corrected. '*Sublimation.*'

Her head snapped around. Coffee cup held out to her, he waited expectantly, his eyes crinkled. Laughing, she shook her head firmly. 'Liar!' She took the cup from him and transferred her attention to it. Maybe things had changed. She couldn't quite meet Zan's dancing gaze, or hold it once she met it, anyway. It was as if their eyes were speaking a different, deeper language than their words.

'Mmm,' he agreed wordlessly. 'She doesn't have a name. She's just a rental boat, nobody's darling.'

'Well, we'll have to name her, then. But won't she interfere with your writing?' She took another sip of coffee and stole another hungry look at him.

Zan shook his head thoughtfully. 'Nope. I think she's just what we need. We can get out of our cage here, work off some steam, and I can think at the same time. I plan to let you do the sailing, while I sit back and meditate.'

'But, Zan, I can't sail.' She shook her hair back nervously, and stared around the boat—so many lines, cleats, unknown devices!

He grinned. 'Anyone who can drive a Porsche can sail a boat. All it takes is practice. And that you're going to get, sweet.' It was hard to say if that was threat or promise.

Threat or promise, Zan made good on it in the next two weeks. When they weren't writing, they were sailing. And it was as easy as he'd said. Within a few days it was Jade who took the helm as they glided around the harbour. While Zan leaned back, his eyes wide and dreaming, she picked the course and gloried in the chuckle of water past the sleek hull, the taut and snowy curve of the jib, the wind in her hair and the sun in her eyes. It was lovely. She loved to sail in the mornings when the wind was light. Gliding slowly along the waterfront, she had time to look up and admire Newport, to savour its stone and clapboard stair-step climb to the green trees, the white and red church steeples that crowned its hill. Or, tiring of the town, she could watch the fishing boats unload at the docks beneath clouds of wheeling seagulls, or tack in close to the sleek whale-shapes of the twelve-metre yachts where they hung in slings with tireless crews polishing their bottoms. Afternoons, when the wind roared in off the ocean from the south-west, she had to keep her eyes on her course as they charged across the harbour, dodging moored and moving boats like a midget ballerina caught in a game of pro football. Either way, she loved it.

For now, Zan's writing was progressing as smoothly as Jade's sailing skills. They had started work on a flashback the day she returned, and apparently Zan knew exactly what he wanted here, had been planning this part of the book for months.

'But what has the 1934 America's Cup match between *Endeavour* and *Rainbow* got to do with your murders in 1980?' Jade wondered, looking up from her writing. And where had she heard the name *Endeavour* before? They had worked dutifully on the patio all morning, till Zan declared a break for lunch and sailing. They'd dropped their sails and picked up a mooring under the lee of Fort Adams while they ate the picnic she had packed, and then inspiration had struck, and Jade found herself scribbling away in the notebook Zan carried for such emergencies. Now it seemed to be fading away again as Zan lounged silently across from her, his thick lashes shutting out distractions, his head propped on the cockpit edge and his long legs stretched out before him. Perhaps he'd gone to sleep on her. 'Hmm?' she prodded.

'Hush. I'm thinking,' he murmured peaceably.

She scowled at his brooding profile and settled back to wait, wishing she'd brought a sketch pad. She'd yet to draw Zan, much less paint him. She looked around. The sky over the fort was bleaching in the hazy sunlight, fading from pale blue to fuzzy white. Far off she heard the bray of a ship's horn, then fainter still, its echo. There was fog out on the ocean today. Even now it was creeping up the channel, throwing hungry tendrils across the hill above the fort as it reached for the harbour.

Zan sat up suddenly. 'No good,' he announced in disgust, taking the pad from her. Standing, he stretched like a big cat, then stepped forward to duck into the crawl space he called a cuddy cabin, where they kept a cooler and the sails. Turning back again, he handed her a dripping green bottle.

'Beer in the afternoon?' She raised an eyebrow.

'We've worked hard today. I'll start again this evening.' Zan lounged back across from her and shut his eyes again, sipping thoughtfully.

Jade drank her beer and studied his face, pondering his writing and this mysterious flashback. This last two weeks had been like a flashback, come to think of it. After an uneasy start, they had fallen back into their early easy, teasing companionship. And the only needs Zan had voiced were for typing and help in the kitchen. Perhaps that night in town had been a fluke, some mysterious moon tide of the masculine psyche which had since ebbed. Only once in a while, when she looked up suddenly, did she surprise a yearning look in those ice-grey eyes. And that was surely not so surprising. He was a man who liked his women, after all, no doubt about that.

Suddenly depressed, Jade swallowed the last of her beer and looked around again. She blinked. Across the cove, the condominium was gone, as was the town beyond. The nearby fort looked soft and dark through the swirling mist. Above, the sky curved brilliant white as it smothered the sun. 'Zan!'

'Hmm, sweet?' He sat up at the note of alarm in her voice and looked around. 'Hmm,' he murmured thoughtfully.

The automatic foghorn off the end of the fort awoke just then to sing out its French-horn warning. Zan's head swung to follow the sound, lifted as it came again. 'Nice,' he said softly. He turned back and his mouth curved slightly as he saw her face. 'No problem, sweet. I can find the way home if we need to.' He rubbed his knuckle slowly across his lips as he watched her, his eyes wide and unblinking.

'You're sure?' Jade stared beyond him into the white shroud, her nerves prickling. It was eerie. The horizon was gone now, sea and sky melting into a white and shimmering bubble around them.

'Mm-hmm.' There was no doubt in Zan's low, smiling voice. 'We can either follow the shoreline around, or sail from mooring to mooring, Jade. I know all the boats in the cove by now. But let's give it half an hour and see if it clears.'

'Okay.' If Zan said he could get her back, then he could. But she was frightened all the same. She slid slowly down to lie on her bench, her knees up, and threw an arm across her eyes to shut out the blinding white. Was it the fog that scared her, or being trapped alone with Zan? She lay quietly and listened to the foghorn. Far away a ship bellowed mournfully.

'And what does the horn say to you?' Zan's warm voice floated out of her darkness, making her feel colder, even more alone . . . Beneath her arm, she tried to smile.

'Say? It doesn't say. It's a colour, Zan, and a shape. Hollow, reaching curves of blue-violet.'

He laughed softly. 'The difference between an artist and a writer, that . . .'

'What does it say to you?' she asked at last.

He waited until the signal came round again. 'Waaant . . .' he sang softly with it. 'Waaant . . .' He laughed quietly again as she shuddered. 'You asked, sweet,' he reminded her. 'It comes on late at night sometimes. I wake up in my big empty bed to hear it crying . . . can't get back to sleep.'

'What do you do then?' she asked faintly. Beneath her arm she squeezed her eyes tight, hurting and not sure why.

'Get up, get a glass of wine, and bring it back to bed . . . Lie back against the pillows, there in the dark, and drink it, staring out towards the bridge.' His breath hissed harshly. 'Beats howling at the moon.' He took another breath. 'I used to get up and write, or run when it got like that, but not this summer.'

'I'm sorry.' Jade's voice came out so tiny, she wondered if he heard it.

'It'll heal.' His low words held something warmer and kinder than a smile. 'It'll heal.'

After a moment, she heard him slide down on his bench beside her and sigh. She fought the urge to reach out and touch his shoulder. Why did she have to feel this overwhelming need to comfort him, to fill his loneliness? If he was lonely, it was self-imposed, wasn't it? Just part of his writer's discipline. And if Zan made the rules, he could break them, couldn't he, if they grew too painful? A phone call would surely bring Irena, or Mona, or probably any one of a dozen other girls from his address book running. So it was his choice, to be alone. And none of her business.

'What's it like, Jade, being in love?' The low voice beside her was whimsical, lightly amused.

Dropping her arm, she turned to gape at him. Head pillowed on his good arm, Zan stared up at the fog, his clear eyes reflecting the white sky. 'What do you mean?' she asked finally.

The corner of his mouth quirked faintly. 'I mean exactly that. What's it like?'

Was he *serious*? Surely this was one of Zan's jokes. Faithful or not to her, didn't he even love his Mona? 'That's a terrible handicap for a writer, I'd think,' she said lightly at last, 'not to know about love . . . This last fifty pages or so with your blonde heroine, I've thought you've done pretty well . . .'

His head swung to face her. 'You mean the redhead? Don't think I haven't noticed your changing her hair colour, sweet!' His lips twitched. 'I'm just biding my time till the last draft. The author gets the last word . . . But that's not love anyway, that's sex, Jade. Tell me what love's like. Do you go off your feed? Do your ears ring? Are you so absentminded that you jump stop signs?'

Frowning, Jade ignored this last crack, and tried to picture Fred's face. She couldn't, quite.

'Well . . . you want to be with him . . . you're happy when he's happy—' she broke off angrily. 'Oh, come on, Zan, you know what it's like! You've been in love before, even if it didn't last . . .'

'But if it didn't last, it wasn't love, was it?' he asked softly with a child's dreadful logic. 'So what do I know?'

If it didn't last, it wasn't love. The words echoed in her mind like the haunting blue moan of the foghorn and Jade shivered violently, hugging herself. *If it didn't last*—such lonely words! Not just for Zan, who didn't know what love was, but for herself, feeling love fading away like fog before the wind . . .

'You're cold, aren't you, Red?' A big hand slid under her back, lifting her, and Zan settled in behind her. He pulled her back to lean against his shoulder, his arm warm and solid around her waist.

Jade shuddered and lay rigid, too cold and lonely to move, too tense to relax. His chin settled on the top of her head and Zan took a deep, ragged breath, but that was all. No demands this time, only warmth and comfort, and wonderful strength. She closed her eyes and slowly settled back against him, feeling his heartbeat against her shoulder blade.

At last, when she lay limp and peaceful in his hold, his chin moved, rasping softly across her hair. 'Now tell me about the other one,' he murmured in her ear. 'The one before Fred.' His arm tightened as she tried to sit up.

Betrayed, she shook her head against his chin, straining forward. 'There's nothing to tell!'

His soft snort in her ear called her a liar. 'Have you ever told anyone, Jade? Even Fred?'

Slowly she shook her head. In those first months, Fred had known she was hurting, had made every effort to console her, yet somehow she'd never told him. 'No,' she whispered, settling slowly back against his warmth again.

'Well, then there's lots to tell. Tell me.'

'No,' she whispered again.

'Can you reach that picnic basket, sweet?' he asked her. From the corner of her eye she saw him nod at the hamper tucked under the forward end of the bench.

'Not from here,' she murmured, trying to sit up. But his arm still prevented her. 'Why?'

'Never mind. I was just wondering if I'd packed the thumbscrews,' he teased gently. His arm squeezed her and then relaxed again. 'Tell me.'

She shook her head bitterly. 'I was such a fool, Zan.'

'Being a fool's a God-given right till you're twenty-five or so. It might even be a goddam duty. How old were you?' With his chin resting on her head, his deep voice seemed to bypass her ears, echo inside of her mind.

'Not that young,' she said ruefully. 'It was just over a year ago.'

'Twenty-three, then. That's not terribly ancient.' His smile seemed to form inside her head. With her eyes closed, she could see his eyes crinkle. 'Who was he?'

'A visiting professor—Irish, come to teach a semester at Brown up in Providence.' She tensed, picturing Jack's charming, foxy face, and Zan's arm squeezed her comfortingly.

'And he was married, of course. And he said he was single,' Zan said softly.

'How did *you* know?' She gasped, then scowled as she felt his chest heave with silent laughter. '*Damn* you, let me go, Zan!' she stormed, twisting against his arm, but he only pulled her closer, his cheek rubbing her hair.

'Hush . . . hush, I'm sorry, sweet, I'm sorry! It was laugh or cry, one or the other. I'm sorry.'

Jade held herself stubbornly rigid in his hold, but there was no escaping him. His cheek rubbed her slowly, rasping hypnotic, soothing messages across her hair, and his arm knew when at last the fight went out of her. He soothed her for a while longer and then his head finally stopped. 'And when did you find out?' he prompted gently.

Jade took a deep, shaky breath. He was going to have it all, every bit of it. Zan didn't even need the thumb-screws. She might as well get it over and be done with it. 'The night I was going to . . . to . . .' she floundered to a halt.

'Try "sleep with him",' he offered dryly. 'There're better words, but that'll do.'

She nodded against his chin. 'He'd opened a bottle of champagne . . .'

'An original bastard,' Zan commented bitterly, 'and then?'

'His . . . wife walked in. She was a model, English, I think, working down in New York—had just driven up for a surprise visit. She was beautiful, and as hard as nails. She looked me up and down, said his taste was improving, and asked if he was still recommending Ireland for the honeymoon.'

'You were talking *marriage*?' Zan exploded behind her, his arm compressing her ribs.

She had to fight for the air to say it. 'Of . . . course we were! I thought I was in love, and he was a liar!' She chewed her lip and tasted blood, as Zan shook his head slowly back and forth against her hair.

'Silly sweet,' he murmured tenderly. 'Why do you have to be so serious? You can play around without thinking it's love every time, Jade.'

Her eyes filled slowly with tears. Was that Zan's formula for success?

'And what happened then?' His voice echoed in her head.

'She . . . went upstairs. I turned to go and he stopped me at the front door, told me she'd be gone in a few days, and we could . . . get on with it.' Jade took a breath. 'I let him have it, and he . . . hit me back.'

'Open-handed or closed?' Zan's voice grated in her ear.

The question was so typically male that she had to laugh. But it didn't come out as laughter. 'I don't know, Zan, I never saw it coming!' she hiccuped, leaning back against his neck. 'I saw stars! I woke up at the bottom of the steps, with the door shut. End of affair. End of story.'

He was absolutely still, his chin pressing down against the top of her head, his heart hammering against her back. 'He's not still in the States, is he?' he asked hopefully at last.

It did come out as laughter this time. Jade turned quickly and brushed her lips against his shirt sleeve. 'No, Zan, he isn't. You can't bash him for me. But thank you.'

He growled something into her hair and pulled her closer, and with the foghorn moaning through the mist, they sat like that for a long time, filled with an emotion too fragile to question or even acknowledge.

At last, Jade lifted her head. Was the mist thinning a little? The dark blur ahead of them marked the nearby shore, but the fog swirled a deepening grey now, not white. 'It's going to be dark soon, Zan. Hadn't we better go?'

'Mmm,' he agreed, the sound muffled against the back of her neck. 'In a minute. Just tell me one more thing?'

'What?'

'Tell me how lover boy came along and picked up the pieces?' His arm tightened as she stiffened and he corrected himself. 'Fred! I mean Fred.'

But she shook her head angrily. 'He didn't pick up the pieces!' she snapped, jerking futilely against his arm. Trust Zan to get around to knocking Fred!

'Well, caught on the rebound, if you prefer,' Zan offered without a trace of remorse, 'though I would have thought that amateur archaeologists were better at collecting pieces than basketballs.'

Teeth gritted, Jade didn't even try to answer that one. Dammit, it hadn't been like that, had it? She'd known and dated Fred before Jack, even turned down his proposal once. And in the months after Jack, Fred's kind and unselfish friendship had pulled her through. They had grown closer, but she had thought of him as friend, not lover. It wasn't until this spring, until her lovely, foolish mother had run off to California, that Jade had finally come to her senses.

'Ol' Fred just lucked out, didn't he?' Zan pressed on

relentlessly. 'A nice, steady, presentable guy—he must have looked awfully safe after that skunk of an Irishman, didn't he?' He gave her a little shake. 'Hmm?'

'Dammit, Zan, it wasn't like that!' she exploded, writhing inwardly as she twisted in his hold, her hair blowing across her face to half blind her. Her mother had abandoned Jade's kind, loving, unspectacular father for a flashy, shallow, golden boy. And suddenly it had come to her—here she was, doing the same! For three years she had been ignoring a sane and constant love, chasing after flashy fakes like a child chasing rainbows while the real thing was in her grasp already. Some people could be fools for a lifetime, missing love in their search for love. She would not be. Fred and she could make something good together . . .

'Must have been mighty soothing to your poor little battered ego,' Zan taunted in her ear, 'to say "yes" to a guy who'd appreciate you—who probably couldn't believe his luck in getting you, who'd worship the ground you walk on? Right? Wasn't that how it was?' His voice was tighter, harsher than she had ever heard it before as he shook her again.

She gave up trying to escape and twisted to face him instead. His arm loosened enough to permit this and she found herself glaring up into icy, blazing eyes.

'No!' she snapped. 'It wasn't like that at all! I just realised I loved him!'

'*Love* him? You don't know the meaning of the word!' Zan laughed bitterly. 'Love is being happy when he's happy,' he quoted her smarmily. 'What about the other side of love, Jade? The hellish side? What about the green-eyed monster that claws at your guts, when your love smiles for someone else? The feeling when you wake up in a bed too big for one, and she's nowhere in reach? You don't know about that yet, do you, sweetheart? I've been watching you this summer, Jade, and if you're missing your Fred, you're hiding it pretty damn well! I think you're loving with your head, not your heart!'

'Stop it!' she gasped, her green eyes gleaming with tears.

He pressed on remorselessly. 'There have been only a few times this summer that I've wondered, only once, really, that I've seen your look like a woman in love, and that was that night at the restaurant, when you were thinking about your engagement.'

That night at the restaurant . . . when she'd been thinking about *Zan*, about the kind of lover he'd be . . . Jade shuddered and felt the blood wash through her cheeks like a spring tide as her mind cried out in protest. No! she thought. No, I won't be such a fool! She stared up at him wordlessly.

He studied her mercilessly for an endless minute, his fingers biting into her waist. 'Well, perhaps you have convinced yourself that you're in love, Red,' he murmured thoughtfully at last. 'But I suggest you think again. It doesn't quite ring true, somehow. And you haven't convinced me, yet . . . quite.'

Leaning back against his arm, trapped in his hold and trapped by an emotion that was struggling for recognition, calling for its name, Jade shook back her hair and widened her glittering eyes. 'Then what will it take to convince you?' she snarled. And what would it take to convince herself again? Zan was ruining everything!

But her anger just seemed to amuse him. He wasn't smiling yet, but the lines were crinkling out from the corners of his wide eyes. 'How about a kiss?' he suggested gravely, his eyes dancing. 'If you love Fred that much, a kiss from me should leave you cold. Perhaps that would convince me?'

Her heart turned over at the thought as her eyes flew to the hard lips above her. 'That proves nothing!' she flung out contemptuously, masking her fear with more anger. 'That's just chemistry—sex! Love's another thing.'

The ice-grey eyes above her narrowed. 'And you're so experienced, Red—you think you know the difference?' he taunted, a smile edging into the low voice.

'Better than you do, apparently!' she lashed out, feeling his trap closing, but not sure of its direction yet nor how to dodge it.

'Oh, *really*?' he purred, as his grin flashed at last. 'Good. Then tell me which this is, Red—love or sex?'

His arm tightened as she leaned away and ducked her head, squinching her eyes like a child waiting for the firecracker to blow, but nothing happened. Jade could feel his breath warm on her jaw, feel the heat of his face leaning above her, but still the kiss didn't fall. She took a shuddering breath, feeling like a fool with her eyes shut. What was he doing, laughing at her? Slowly, cautiously, her eyelashes fluttered open. Still, nothing happened . . . From the corner of her eye, he was a dark mass looming above her. Slowly she turned her head to look up at him, her eyes widening—and his mouth descended. He laughed softly against her lips as his arm slid up to her shoulders and he leaned into her. His mouth moved against hers in a gentle, hypnotic demand that she had no way of denying as her head tilted slowly back under the pressure of his kiss.

Love or sex? he'd asked. As she shuddered and felt her arms sliding up around his neck, Jade knew the answer now. Had known it all along. Love. For her it was love. Her lips parted beneath his, her last defences falling as he took her mouth, tasting it, claiming it, demanding her response, meeting it, then asking for more as he gathered her closer, the cast between them bruising them both.

For her it was love, but what was it for Zan? His breath was rasping her cheeks in a deep and ragged rhythm now and he groaned softly against her face.

What was this kiss for Zan, Zan with a lover in New York and another in Europe, Zan who said it was all right to play around, that she shouldn't be so serious? Her mouth tamed at last, Zan returned to her lips, tracing them in a hot, damp, featherlight caress that turned to pain as he nipped her bottom lip. She moaned in soft protest and he half laughed, half groaned against her cheek, trailed his lips to her jaw and up to her eyebrow.

'Which is it?' he breathed gleefully, his whisper hot and tickling in her ear.

Jade shuddered and threw her head back to stare up at the fog as his lips burned slowly down the length of her throat, shuddered as the foghorn moaned out the answer—'waaant.' For Zan it was want—want and need and sex—joyful, uncomplicated, and as enduring as the summer mist.

'Which is it?' he whispered against the racing pulse at the base of her throat. His hand released her gently, slid around from her shoulders in a slow caress to find her breast as his lips travelled up her throat again. 'Hmm?' he asked. His thumb found her throbbing nipple, traced it in slow, hypnotic circles.

But, gasping for breath, Jade didn't answer. Wonderful as it was, it wasn't love, and it wouldn't last. And where would that leave her, when Zan's needs and wants were satisfied and his book was done? She leaned slowly back from him, trying to remember how her feet and legs worked, as his mouth came back to her lips again. It left her in pieces, that was where it left her. Pieces too tiny, too scattered, for even the most patient of archaeologists to bother with.

Jade pushed down hard, forcing herself up and away from his startled grasp. Staggering backwards, she caught her balance and stared down at him, her body throbbing with its own demands for his touch.

Silently Zan looked up at her, his wide eyes caressing

her flushed face and touseled hair with obvious satisfaction. 'Well, Red,' he asked at last, cocking his head slightly, 'which was that, do you think—love or sex?'

It was almost possible to hate him, Jade thought dizzily, for what he was doing to her. She edged one foot backwards. The cockpit was too small for them both. The *boat* was too small.

Zan stood up smoothly. 'You're not sure yet?' he teased, laughter warm in his low voice as he reached for her. 'Well, let's try the other kiss. Maybe it'll be clearer then.'

His hand slid slowly up her bare arm, but she jerked herself free and backed away. 'Zan, don't touch me again!'

His head lifted. 'Why not, sweet?' he demanded, his gold brows bunching with the question.

Because one more kiss would finish her, would rob her of every last bit of sense and resistance she could command. 'Because I love Fred!' she lied desperately, backing away another step.

Zan shook his head. 'Liar. I don't believe you,' he said softly, taking a step forward, his hand outstretched.

Her eyes never leaving him, Jade stepped up on to the seat. The little boat rocked gently. 'Zan, you touch me again, and I'll jump over the side!' she vowed.

His eyes crinkled in amusement. 'I don't believe you,' he repeated tauntingly, his hand stretching out towards her with the slow, hypnotic stealth of a child reaching for a flower-drunk butterfly.

She shot a glance over her shoulder at the water, then turned back again, her eyes flashing. He was closer. 'Zan!'

As her weight shifted, the laughter in his widening eyes flickered and went out. 'Jade!' He snatched at her, his hand just grazing her waist as she twisted away and dived, and wet darkness closed over the daylight.

'Ho!' It has no right to be this cold! Jade thought as she

burst to the surface, gasping. She ducked under to throw the hair back from her face and came up again, panting with the cold. 'Oh!'

'Jade! Get over here!' Zan kneeled on the seat, his hand outstretched and his eyes blazing. Seen from the water, he looked enormous.

It was too cold to tread water and argue. And she might as well complete the gesture, now she'd started it. Jade shook her head. 'No, thanks, Zan! I'm swimming ashore.' Turning away from the boat, she struck out, swimming rapidly to fight the chill. It wasn't far.

'Jade! It's further than it looks! Come back here!' He'd never sounded like that before, rage and some-thing else rasping in the harsh command. A shaft of fear shot through her with the cold. She'd pushed him too far this time. She couldn't go back now. And she had to keep moving. Her strokes lengthened.

'*Jade*!' he yelled once more. The emotion in his voice chilled her more than the salt water slopping over her head as a wave passed. She choked and kicked harder, and began to feel the drag of her light clothing.

Behind her she heard cursing and the light, metallic scrape of the sail clips sliding up the mast as Zan raised the mainsail. He could do it all by himself, the single hand just slowed him down.

Treading water, Jade lifted her head to study the shore. It was getting closer now, but it seemed to slid away to her left. The tide must be ebbing out of the harbour and into the bay, sucking the water out and down to the waiting sea, taking her with it. She started swimming again, harder now, as behind her the jib fluttered up its stay. He'd be under way in another minute, but she was swimming directly into the light breeze. Zan would have to tack twice to catch her.

Her breath was coming harder, and the cold water growing heavier. She could make out individual rocks along the shore now, but to her right she could also see the end of the point, the mouth of the channel, looming up through the fog. The current would run swifter there as it turned the corner. And Zan would kill her if he caught her now. A wave smashed into her face . . . If she didn't drown first! She forgot about Zan and began to swim for her life.

For an endless, freezing time Jade swam through the dusk with the darker shore hanging beyond like a broken promise and the foghorn at the end of the point sounding closer and closer each time it moaned. Where was Zan? Her feet grazed the bottom and then lost it as the current sucked at her again. She gagged as she inhaled a wave, and the foghorn's cry curved over her. It was now or never. Throwing her arms out before her, she lunged against the tide, kicking frantically. Her foot grazed bottom. She would make it after all!

She staggered ashore at a launching ramp, the concrete cold and slimy beneath her bare feet. Shivering, she turned back to the water. Pale in the gauzy twilight, the little boat reached slowly in from the point, paralleling the shore, a dark figure standing at the helm. Jade felt a sudden rush of warmth as her eyes blurred. So he'd been guarding her all this time. If the current had won, Zan would have been there at the point to meet her.

As the boat neared, their eyes met across fifty feet of water and her warmth faded. Jade shivered again. She could read the rage in the frozen lift of his head, didn't need to see those grey eyes to feel the ice in them. Suddenly she was infinitely grateful that Zan could not reach her, that there was no way to beach the deep-keeled sailboat.

Wordless, they stared at each other as the boat glided past. Zan moved his hand and the sloop turned in a slow graceful gybe and floated away across the cove. For a moment it seemed to hang, a pale moth in the grey air, then it was gone. Jade shivered and started the long walk home.

Her guardian angel was working over time that evening: a patrolling police car picked her up just past the fort and delivered her to her doorstep with a scathing lecture on the follies of swimming alone in the fog; her keys were still in the pocket of her shorts; and Zan was not on her doorstep. Not yet. She staggered in at the back door and into the shower, her mind as numb as her body.

What a fool she'd been! Not just this evening, although that was the stupidest stunt she'd ever pulled, but all summer! She should have taken one look at Zan and run for her life—left him lying in the road if need be. Fool, to think that the only danger Zan represented was financial ruin! She had let him spoil everything. Nothing would ever be the same, after Zan.

The phone rang and Jade scurried across the kitchen, her towel flapping, and scooped the receiver up.

'Red?' Zan's low voice rasped into her ear, and she sank to the mattress, smiling in spite of herself. 'Are you there, you flaming turkey?' he snarled.

'Yes,' she whispered.

'You moron,' he began carefully, taking a deep breath. It was the nicest thing he called her in the next few minutes, as she received the full barrage of a considerable and creative vocabulary. At the very least, it drove out the last of her chill as she huddled on the bed with scorching ears. Finally, Zan ran out of wind, if not out of invention. His breath hissed against her ear. 'You still there?' he asked huskily.

'Yes,' she whispered.

There was a moment of awkward silence.

'You all right?' he asked at last.

'Yes, Zan, I am.' She groped for a matter-of-fact tone and nearly got it right. 'Are *you* okay? You sound . . . funny.'

He snorted. 'Well, I damn well *feel* funny! I've had two drinks in the last twenty minutes and my hands still haven't stopped shaking!'

'I'm sorry . . .'

'I should damn well hope you're sorry! There's easier ways to tell a man you don't want his loving than drowning yourself, sweetheart. Try "no, thank you", next time. It's dryer!'

'I'm sorry—I thought I tried that.'

'Did you?' He sighed. 'Guess I missed it in all the excitement, sweet. Try a winch handle, then, next time. But *don't* go over the side . . .'

'I'm sorry,' she repeated humbly.

'So am I,' Zan growled. 'And I'll be a damn sight sorrier if my hair's gone white. I'm scared to go and look in the mirror!'

Suddenly, the urge to see him was overwhelming. Jade squeezed the receiver until her knuckles cracked. 'You don't . . . want to work any tonight, do you, Zan?' she asked wistfully.

His breath rasped in her ear, and she could imagine his gold head lifting dangerously as the icy eyes narrowed. 'Jade,' he said softly, 'I have never beaten a woman in my life before, and I'd like to keep it that way. I suggest you stay out of my sight until tomorrow. Clear enough?'

'Y-yes,' she whispered.

'Goodnight, then.'

''Night, Zan, I'm—' the phone clicked in her ear, and her eyes filled with tears. '—sorry,' she finished.

CHAPTER EIGHT

AND Jade was even sorrier in the following days, as Zan paid her back for his scare and his wounded pride. She might as well have been a dictaphone for all the attention he gave her, and the only words passed between them were the dictation of his story. It was more painful than she would have imagined, to be deprived of his teasing, offhand affection, and it was a frightening forecast of how she would feel when Zan was gone at last.

His ill-humour seemed to be affecting his writing as well, for the book was grinding to a halt. It took Jade almost a week to realise this, as Zan rattled out page after page of material. All of it was good, some of the passages even brilliant to her admittedly prejudiced eyes, and none of it fitted together. Like a smashed mirror the pieces gleamed brilliant and razor-sharp, but the story they should have reflected was fractured and lost.

And yet Zan would admit nothing. His tanned face grew harder and blanker day by day, and he drove them both ruthlessly as he searched for a path through the blizzard of words he was producing. That or he sat on the end of the dock for hours, unmoving, unhearing, staring out at the harbour, only to come back to her with more false starts, dead ends, and fragments.

And so how would Zan be this morning? Jade wondered, as she hurried down the hill. Yesterday, she had made the mistake of suggesting he take a break, perhaps catch the train to New York for some well-needed rest and recreation. His reception of that suggestion had been almost savage—it was here that the problem was, and here that he would face it, he had informed her with tight-jawed, brittle control. But by noon, Zan had simply given up the struggle. He had quietly picked up the morning's typing, dropped it in the trash can, and told her to come back the next day. Scooping up a six-pack of beer out of the fridge, he had stalked down the dock to the sailboat, and looking at his face, Jade had not dared ask him to go along.

She glanced at her watch. If Zan was still out of temper, her tardiness certainly wasn't going to help matters. She had awakened to the cry of the foghorn sometime around three last night, had lain for hours listening to the lonely moans across the bay, wondering if Zan could sleep, or if he was as lonely this night as she was. When she woke again, it was late; a grey and fuzzy light shone through the herbs at the window above the sink. She had overslept.

And then, as she had hurried out of the back door, an anxious Cathy had delayed her to give her a letter from Fred. It had arrived the day before and Cathy had accidentally taken it upstairs, tucked inside an advertising circular. Thanking her hurriedly, Jade had jammed the unread letter into her jeans pocket and dashed away. She was quite late now, and Zan would surely be angry. Well, serve him right for deserting her yesterday!

But Zan didn't answer her knock at the door, and Jade waited, frowning. Surely he was up by now? Perhaps out back? Unlocking the door, she walked in. Silence . . . She stepped lightly across the oak floor, heading for the patio, but glanced down into the sunken living room. Zan lay sprawled out on the sofa below her, fast asleep.

Sucking in her breath in quiet appreciation, Jade stood mesmerised. He was so beautiful lying there, bare but for a pair of khaki shorts pulled low around his lean waist. Only the bulky cast marred the grace of that big, muscular body. His golden head was turned away from her into his good arm, the cord in the tanned column of his neck standing out in bold relief. What would it be like to touch him, to follow that line down into the curly gold at the base of his throat, to slide her hands across the hard muscles of his wide chest?

'Jade?' Zan murmured. Frowning, he swung his head slowly towards her, then stopped, his thick lashes brushing his cheeks. 'That you, sweet?'

Jade whirled completely around to inspect the bare wall, her face flaming. Thank *God* he hadn't opened his eyes, just then! 'Mm-hmm,' she answered.

'What . . . time is it?' he muttered indistinctly.

Jade turned around again, her embarrassment forgotten. 'Zan, are you okay?' She bounded down into the pit.

At closer glance, there were deep shadows under the gold lashes, and stubble roughened his lean jaw. She sank down on the edge of the sofa beside him. 'Are you all right?' Brushing his silky hair back, she laid a hand on his forehead.

'Mmm. Fine now.' He nestled against her hand, smiling drowsily. 'Just don't rock the sofa.'

He didn't seem to have a fever. She stared down at him, scowling anxiously. 'Let's see your eyes, Zan,' she ordered.

The thick lashes lifted slowly, and she felt him frown beneath her hand. 'Ouch,' he murmured, squinting up at her with bloodshot eyes.

Jade inhaled sharply. 'You—are—hung over, Alexander Wykoff!' she diagnosed indignantly.

'Who's that?' he queried serenely, shutting his eyes again, but he grabbed for her hand as she removed it. 'Wait! Where are you going?'

'I'm going to get you some aspirin and coffee, unless you prefer to sleep it off?'

'No. Sounds good . . . hurry back.' He rolled over on his side and cuddled into a cushion.

Jade scowled as she brewed the coffee. Zan was amusing, hung over, but the situation was not. She'd known him nearly two months now, and had never seen him drunk, nor even close to it before. He'd taken more than a six pack of beer yesterday to get in this shape. She chewed her lip. He had to snap out of this!

Setting the coffee tray on an end table, Jade sat down beside Zan. His eyes fluttered open again.

'Aspirin time,' she declared firmly. 'Sit up, Zan.'

With a soft groan he rolled over on to his good elbow and half sat, blinking owlishly.

Jade stared at him, half amused, half exasperated. Propped on his left arm like that, he couldn't hold a glass. Oh, well. Who had crippled him in the first place? 'Open up,' she said briskly.

Balancing the aspirin carefully on his dry, pink tongue, Jade picked up the water glass and eyed him doubtfully. How best to do this? Leaning against his chest, she slid her left hand behind his neck, up into his warm, thick hair to support his head. She tried not to shiver as his warmth spread in slow, electric waves across her body. Carefully, her face sternly impersonal, she put the glass to his lips. Zan swallowed obediently, his eyes on her face as he drank.

'Enough?' she asked.

His lips quivered, then straightened again. 'No,' he said. 'More.' He drank the whole glass slowly, watching her the while with hungry, laughing eyes. Feeling her face colour, Jade didn't know whether to scowl or to laugh at his satisfaction.

Finally she set the empty glass aside. Head tilted back against her hand, Zan waited, his eyes on her lips. It would be so easy to just dip her head, brush that long, mobile mouth with her own . . . 'Coffee?' she asked abruptly.

He shook his head slowly, his eyes telling her what he wanted.

'Well, I'm having some.' She pulled her hand gently from behind his neck and turned away. Zan sighed and lay back to stare up at the ceiling.

Jade poured a cup and sat down beside him, the top of his head nearly brushing her thigh. It would be so easy to reach out and stroke his furry chest . . . 'So what happened?' she asked.

Zan smiled, his eyes closing again. 'Not much, really . . . The sail did no good . . . so went over to Jerry's for a drink, got him talkin' . . . More he drinks, more outrageous the stories get, Jade . . .' He stopped and yawned hugely. 'But he won't drink 'less I keep him company . . . 'ol devil's got a hollow leg you wouldn't believe . . .' His brows knotted. 'Not even sure I can remember the best of them now. You have to come and take notes, next time.'

Zan leaned forward suddenly, heaved himself up on his elbow, then slid backwards. His heavy, warm head dropped into her lap. He smiled up at her lazily. 'Long as you're playing nurse, you might as well do it properly,' he explained kindly, shutting his eyes again.

Jade took a deep breath and a good swallow of coffee. *Damn* the man. 'So was that all?' she asked casually, ignoring the invasion.

'No.' Zan frowned. He was silent so long she wondered if he'd gone to sleep on her. 'I got home after midnight . . . went to sleep. I don't know when the foghorns started . . . but before long, all I could hear was those damn horns fillin' the sky. I kept dreamin' it was the last trump sounding, thinking of all the things I'd meant to do and hadn't had the time for . . . There's so little time left and it's going so fast and I'm getting *nowhere* . . .' His head turned restlessly on her leg.

'You mean the book?' she asked softly.

'No, I don't, nimwit, but that's another problem. So I'd roll over, go back to sleep, and hear the horns again—waaant! waant!' He took a deep breath. 'Finally, I got up, got dressed, and walked across to Ocean Drive, watched the fog roll down the channel. I walked back by your house, thought of dragging you out for some typing, but I didn't figure you'd thank me.'

'I'd have come,' she protested.

He smiled, and reaching back, found her knee and held on to it. 'Would you have, sweet?' he asked softly. 'Kicking and screaming, I 'spose you would have,' he decided. 'Anyway, I came home alone, and read the manuscript all the way through, and it rots.'

Jade shook her head. 'No, it doesn't!'

'Yes, it does,' he said evenly. 'At that point I'd have gone out and howled along with the foghorns, but I figured Jerry would call the cops, or the dogcatcher, or both.'

'Poor Zan, you had a tough night,' she murmured soothingly, wishing she could stroke his hair.

He laughed ironically. 'And then the phone rang.'

'Oh?' She set her empty cup down carefully, watching his face.

'It was Mona, calling from London.'

'At that hour?'

His lips twitched. 'It was morning there. But Mona's always had a fine disregard for time zones, anyway.' He shook his head again. 'She made me open a bottle of champagne before she'd talk to me.'

'Champagne?'

'Mmm-hmm.' Zan smiled crookedly. 'She had a bottle there, too. She wanted me to help her toast her new love, be the first one to know about her up-coming marriage.' His hand squeezed her knee suddenly, as if a spasm of pain tightened it, but he grinned. 'I can't decide if I actually *was* the first to know, or the second. He sounded so dazed, I really think she might have forgotten to inform him beforehand.'

'You *talked* to him?' Jade gasped. She could feel the angry blood heating her face. How could the woman have *done* that to Zan?

'Oh, yes,' Zan said dryly. 'She had him right there in

bed with her. An architect. Sounded very nice. Pleased as punch, but somewhat dazed.' He sighed and was silent a long time, his hand absently caressing her kneecap. 'I hope he's all right. The girl has a talent for loving rascals . . . witness me . . .' His lips curled and then straightened again, and he took a slow breath. 'So, after the happy couple rang off, there I sat with the foghorns and half a bottle of champagne going flat. Finally I figured, what the hell, I'd toast my own future . . . dim as it sometimes seems lately. Next thing I knew, here you were . . .' He sighed slowly as his hand relaxed on her knee, and he lay there, thinking or dreaming, she couldn't tell which.

Jade studied his face. Was he sad? The thick golden lashes shut her out, gave away no secrets, but he had to be. However easy-going his relationship with Mona might have been, there was love there, even if Zan didn't call it that. She saw it shine every time he mentioned the woman. And a husband would shut him out as another lover might not.

Zan's head turned restlessly on her thigh and his hand tightened again, sending slow waves of pleasure washing up her leg. Her whole lap glowed with the weight of him. His lashes fluttered open and he smiled up at her, stopping her heart for a beat. 'Go upstairs and go to bed, sleepyhead,' she told him softly. 'We can work tomorrow.'

His smile deepened. 'Will you come keep me company if I do?' he asked drowsily, his fingers exploring the shape of her kneecap.

That would be one way to cheer him up, wouldn't it? Jade thought wryly. She smiled and shook her head.

Zan sighed and shrugged his eyebrows. 'How 'bout a nice cold shower, then?' he coaxed. 'It's a big tub.'

'Go to sleep,' she told him firmly, trying to frown.

Sighing again, he sat up abruptly and swung his long legs to the floor. He leaned over his knees for a moment, suddenly looking ill. 'Nope,' he said. 'It's work time. I'll have a quick shower and then let's get going.'

'Zan—' she protested.

Standing, he poured himself a cup of coffee and looked down at her. 'Jade, we're so far behind now, it isn't funny any more.'

'So what if you're late?' she asked defiantly. He did look ill.

Scowling, he shook the hair out of his eyes and then stopped abruptly, as if the movement hurt. 'Jade, I've taken—and spent—a nice advance . . . We planned this book to hit market just before the America's Cup campaign starts next spring.' He trudged off towards the stairs, carrying his coffee. 'I'm scheduled to start another book in the Bahamas in October.'

Jade bit her lip. Zan in the Bahamas. For the first time, the reality of his leaving Newport went home— went home like an ice-pick. She took a deep, slow breath. 'Breakfast?' she called up after him. Remarkable how steady her voice sounded.

'Later.'

Later . . . she wandered aimlessly around the living room, picked up one of his old sailing books. Sooner or later he'd be gone . . . He'd tossed a sweater on to the hearth; she collected that absently, rubbing it across her face, breathing in the clean, sunny smell of him. Here it was—what—almost August? Two months from now Zan would be in the Bahamas. And she'd be here, watching the leaves turn red and then fall, teaching school, probably married . . . She found two more books on an end table, and his shirt on a dining room chair and started upstairs. What a fool she'd been . . .

She could hear the shower going as she dumped Zan's debris on his bed, and wandered into the guest room. Absently, she picked up a stack of her paintings and began to lay them out across the bed, her eyes unseeing. She focussed as she came to the one she had done of Zan two days ago. He had sat on the wall beneath her balcony, thinking, for nearly two hours, giving her all the time she needed . . .

Hands thrust deep in her pockets, she brooded down at it. It was good—very good. She'd caught his faraway, almost fey look as he stared out at the water . . . And what would she do with this? She couldn't possibly sell it, wouldn't possibly be able to look at it once he was gone . . . She turned away, blinking rapidly, balling her fingers into fists.

A paper crackled against her hand and she fished it out automatically. Fred's letter. Turning towards the harbour, she tore it open absently and then read it, but the words didn't register. She read it again, frowning . . . October. Fred wanted to marry in October now. Columbus Day weekend. The rush of starting school would be behind them, they'd have a long weekend, could honeymoon on Nantucket if she liked . . . In October, Zan would be in the Bahamas.

Jade crumpled the letter into a blue wad as she stared out at the harbour. It was a painting by Monet, the bright colours smearing and blurring. Fool . . . to think that she could pick up the pieces, go on as before, after Zan. Selfish fool, to expect Fred to help her. It wasn't fair; not fair to Fred, not fair to herself. She would have to tell Fred—call it off. A man deserved more than half a heart—was that what her mother had finally realised? Some day she would have to ask her . . . The colours were dripping off the canvas before her, blues and whites and touches of brighter colours swimming and running together. Jade shut her eyes and felt the tears trickle down her cheeks. It wasn't *fair*! Fred loved her, she loved Zan, and who did Zan love? Nobody? Everybody? Mona? Just himself?

'Jade?' From the doorway, his low voice cut through her misery and she jumped violently.

'Hmm?' she managed, squaring her shoulders. He

wouldn't come into this room without her permission. It was an unspoken agreement they had. She stared out at the water, willing him to go away.

'Help me on with this shirt, will you, sweet?' he asked. The doorframe creaked as he leaned against it.

. Jade swallowed carefully. 'In a minute, Zan,' she muttered. Why, oh, why wouldn't the tears stop? She couldn't even lift a hand to wipe them away with him watching.

'Jade?' His voice had sharpened. 'What's the matter?'

'Nothing!' She got it out through clenched teeth. Any second now her shoulders would start shaking; she could feel the heaving in her chest.

'Then turn around and look at me,' Zan demanded.

She shook her head tightly, then stiffened as she heard his footsteps. 'Zan, get *out* of here!' she stormed helplessly. 'This is *my* room!'

'You *are*—you're crying, aren't you, Jade?' His hand closed on her arm, pulling her gently around.

'No!' She jerked away, whirling around again, but his cast hooked around her waist and hauled her back against him, and his other arm completed the circle. She squinched her eyes and leaned back, shuddering, feeling the dampness and the heat of his bare chest seep through her shirt back. The sweetness of his touch made the tears fall faster.

'Hey . . . hey . . . hey, don't cry, sweet, why are you—' Zan's lips brushed the side of her cheek, her neck, her hair, then his head stopped suddenly. 'So that's it,' he said dully.

Jade opened tear-fringed eyes. Dazzled by the damp, clean smell of him and the heat of his arms, she took a second to realise what he was looking at. In front of them, her upflung hand clutched the forgotten letter.

Zan's arm squeezed her painfully. 'Did you just open that?' he asked against her ear, his voice husky.

Jade nodded, shut her eyes and took a deep, sniffling

breath, just wishing she could stand like this for ever.
She nodded again.

'Damn, damn, *damn* then!' he muttered against her
hair as his arms crushed her ribs, 'do you miss him that
much?'

A peal of hysterical laughter exploded in her chest,
came out as a tearing sob, followed by another, and
another. His conclusion was so far off the mark it was
hilarious; why was she crying so?

'Jade . . . Jade . . . oh, *hell*, girl!' Zan turned her
around and pulled her against his chest and she bur-
rowed against him, pressing her face into the damp
curling hair, the hard and comforting warmth of him. He
stroked her hair and rocked her, muttering soothing,
meaningless curses into her ear, and gradually the sobs
slowed . . . slowed . . . and, finally, stopped . . .

Zan's heartbeat against her forehead was the homiest,
most comforting sound she had ever heard. Hypnotised,
she concentrated on that, felt her breath beginning to
come in time with his own deep rhythm.

'Jade, look at me,' he whispered against her hair.

She stiffened. If she looked at him now, he would
know.

'Jade?'

The doorbell rang, and Zan's head came up. 'Oh,
lord,' he said reverently, his arms tightening around her.

It rang again—two longs and a short. Zan heaved a
deep sigh against her and then stepped back, his hand on
her shoulder. She ducked her head and stood there,
longing for his arms again, swaying slightly.

'Jade,' he said urgently, 'I'm afraid we've got
company.' Two longs and a short, the signal came again.
He shook her gently. 'Can you pull yourself together,
Red?' he coaxed. 'Go and wash your face? Hmm?'

She nodded at the floor. Company?

'Okay, then,' he said doubtfully. His hand squeezed
her shoulder and dropped away. 'Come on down when

you're ready.' The doorbell rang again and he padded out of the room, his footsteps heavier and clumsier than they usually sounded.

Who could this be? Jade wondered as she washed her face. Zan had recognised the signal. She couldn't think of anything she'd rather do less than meet some old friend of his right now. She combed her hair out, and then, to kill more time, changed her blouse. Perhaps his visitor would leave if she stalled long enough.

In the mirror, she looked about eighteen, with her freshly-washed face, her jeans and a check shirt. And her eyes were as pink as Zan's now. Well, perhaps it would be assumed that, like Zan, she'd been drinking, rather than crying . . . What a fool she'd made of herself! She hadn't howled like that in years. Reluctantly, she stepped out of the bathroom. She would think about that later.

In the hallway, voices floated up from the pit below. Jade paused, not consciously eavesdropping, but scouting out the approaching encounter.

'No, Zan, I don't think I'll buy that,' a woman's voice purred. 'If you said you'd broken it falling *into* someone's bed, I'd believe you. But falling *out* of bed?' She laughed throatily, and Jade cocked her head. Where had she heard a laugh like that before?

'That won't fly, hmm?' Zan mused. 'Well, give me a few minutes and I'll come up with a better story then. I'm a bit slow this morning.'

'Yes, I'd noticed.' There was a touch of acid behind those dry words. 'You've been drinking, haven't you, Zan?'

'It shows?' he asked ironically.

But she took him seriously. 'Darling, *everything* shows after thirty! Haven't you learned that by now?' She chuckled tenderly. 'Besides, I know that little-boy-lost look only too well . . . Now, where's this famous secretary of yours?'

Biting her lip, Jade turned towards the stairs. Might as well get this over with. Something told her it would not be pleasant. She walked down the stairs, her eyes wide and wary, her chin high, and as she turned at the bottom step, her gaze locked with that of the woman in the living room.

Jade had a fleeting impression of steely blue eyes in a pale, exquisitely made up face, of eyebrows plucked too thin. The eyebrows arched and frowned delicately as the blue eyes narrowed. 'Zan,' the woman murmured. The name held a world of weary disgust.

From the corner of her eye, Jade saw Zan stand. She could feel his eyes on her face as he made the introductions, but pride forced her to return the icy appraisal she was still enduring.

'Irena Adams, this is Jade Kinnane. Irena is my agent,' Zan explained rapidly.

And also his old lover, and also *extremely* angry, Jade realised as she studied the blonde before her. Angry, but icily self-controlled as she lounged back on the sofa, her arms draped gracefully over its back. Beneath a white linen suit which would have paid Jade's mortgage for the summer, her long legs were carefully displayed. And her gaze was just as calculating as her pose as she examined Jade openly.

At last her sleek head turned to Zan. 'The secretarial pool is so low around here that you had to resort to cradle robbing?' she purred sweetly.

Jade felt a flame light in her eyes, and her chin lifted. The day had been bad enough so far. She didn't have to take this.

But behind her, Zan was answering, his voice lazily amused. 'When they're big enough, they're old enough . . . to type, that is, Irena.'

'Mmm.' The blue eyes turned back to rake Jade's face. 'How many words per minute *do* you type, Miss Kinnane?' A thin eyebrow arched sceptically.

Slipping her hands into her pockets, Jade leaned back on her heels with unconscious, arrogant grace and stared down at the woman before her. At least she had the advantage of height at the moment, if not venom. 'I haven't the foggiest,' she drawled gently. But she felt her cheeks beginning to burn.

Zan broke in smoothly. 'You'll have to forgive that question, Jade. Irena has a financial stake in my writing. Sometimes that makes her a bit . . . anxious.'

But that verbal slap was not enough to quell the other woman. She turned to smile at Zan, her eyes wide. 'And how far along *are* you, Zan?' she cooed.

Jade turned to watch his face. Zan was rubbing a knuckle slowly across his lips, his eyes holding Irena's. 'Chapter eleven,' he said bluntly.

'*That's* what I was afraid of.' Irena's smile was grim. 'May I see it?'

Zan's hesitation was barely perceptible. '. . . If you wish,' he said evenly. 'How long are you staying, Irena?'

Irena's blue eyes shifted thoughtfully to Jade's tense face, then slid away again. 'As long as you'll have me, darling,' she purred. 'As long as it takes to get you back on the track.'

Zan's brows twitched. 'All right. Let's get you settled upstairs, and then we'll take you out to lunch, for starters.'

But Irena's brows arched again. 'Lunch *out*? In the middle of a book? This is the man who never mixes business with his pleasure?'

Zan smiled gently, but apparently he had no comeback to this gibe. He turned to Jade, his eyes probing her frozen face. 'Jade, you're going to have to give up your studio for a few days. Want to get on with it?'

'Right!' Jade was only too glad to retreat from this verbal sparring match. The air between Zan and Irena fairly crackled with tension. She was nothing but an unwilling observer, an intruder at this electric reunion.

Jade was clearing the bureau in the guest room when Zan appeared with a suitcase. She picked up a stray tube of paint, tightened its top and fitted it carefully into her kit.

'Jade.' He loomed beside her, his long hand tapping nervously on the bureau top.

Jade studied her kit. The blues were out of order; she needed more Hooker's green. 'Hmm?' she murmured, trying not to bite at her lip.

'Why were you crying like that, Red?' he demanded intensely. '*Look* at me!'

'Zan?' The throaty call from the corridor spared her the trouble of finding a lie.

Zan sighed. 'In here, Irena.'

'What a view!' Irena swept into the room and past them to study the harbour, her long body posing elegantly against the light.

Jade snatched up her brushes and fitted them one by one into their bambo mat holder, rolling them up carefully.

'Yes, it's not bad,' Zan agreed.

As she collected her drawing pencils, Jade could feel Irena turning back towards them.

'And how's the view from *your* room, Zan?' the blonde asked huskily.

There was a moment of vibrating silence before Zan answered—time enough for Jade's teeth to rake her lip. 'Even better,' he answered deliberately.

Jade didn't look up, didn't need to raise her head to see the look passing between them. She collected the brushes, the pencils, the erasers, put them in place and shut the kit.

As if that answer had settled a question, Irena suddenly became brisk. 'All right, Zan, out of here!' she ordered gaily. 'I've got to change.' Shooing him out the door, she closed it and strolled over to the closet.

All at once, the room seemed tiny. *She had to get out*

of here. Jade folded the newspapers up carefully, trying to work quickly and yet look at ease.

'I see you're engaged,' Irena observed behind her.

'Yes.' Jade stuffed the newspapers into the trash can and discovered a stray tube of paint.

'Your fiancé must be *very* self-confident young man, to let you work for Zan Wykoff.'

Jade looked up. In the mirror above the bureau, Irena was smiling widely at her, her fine teeth just showing between the red lips as she unbuttoned her silk blouse. Beneath the blouse she wore a bra as elegant as the breasts it supported. Jade wondered absently if she herself would look that good in ten years. She met Irena's eyes deliberately. 'He's not worried,' she lied lightly. She noted that it hadn't even occurred to his agent that Zan and she might be engaged. That notion was just too preposterous, apparently.

Irena laughed deep in her throat. 'Well, he should be! Zan collects hearts like a collie collects cockleburrs!' Strolling over to the mirror beside Jade, she turned her head to study the smooth twist of blonde hair at the nape of her neck. Not a hair was out of place.

Jade didn't bother to answer that as she refastened the kit. She turned to the bed and began to stack the paintings she had laid out this morning.

'That won't be necessary,' Irena murmured kindly.

Jade looked up blankly, then blazed scarlet as she met Irena's smiling gaze and her meaning hit home. Of course—Irena would not be needing this bed. There was one with a better view, a much better view, next door. 'All the same,' she shrugged, turning back to her work. She reached for the portrait of Zan.

'Why, that's rather clever!' Irena's charmed surprise fell just short of insult as she slithered into a low-cut white sundress.

'Thanks.' Jade set a seascape on top of it and reached for another.

'What will you take for it?'

Jade met her eyes. 'It's not for sale.' And there was no point in giving some lie as to why it was not for sale. They were too in tune. Irena knew why. Jade slipped the paintings into a small portfolio and fastened it carefully, turned to collect her kit.

'Miss Kinnane?' Picking up her handbag, Irena put a hand on the doorknob and turned back to smile at Jade. 'Let me give you just one piece of advice.'

Chin raised, Jade met her eyes. 'I don't believe I asked for any,' she commented wryly.

Irena ignored that. 'Just don't take him seriously.' Her smile widened slowly, lazily, but it never reached the cold eyes. 'For your own sake.' Opening the door, she swayed out into the corridor and Jade followed.

Dressed in slacks and a knit shirt, Zan waited for them at the foot of the stairs. The shadows under his grey eyes gave him a fine-drawn Byronic look which caught at Jade's heart, as he looked up at her. She looked away. He ought to be sleeping.

'Where shall we take Irena for lunch?' he asked quietly.

'Take her to the Pier,' Jade suggested, walking across to the kitchen to collect her sandals.

'You're coming too,' Zan stated firmly.

She slipped on her shoes and looked up at him, tossing back her braid. 'I'm not in the mood today, Zan. I'd rather not.'

'And I'd rather you did.' His jaw tightened.

Why was he trying to be nice about this? It just made things worse. Or perhaps he was using her to tease Irena? 'And *I'd* rather *not*,' she clipped out, her eyes beginning to blaze even as she smiled up at him.

'Zan, don't be a tyrant!' Irena interrupted, laughing. She slipped a hand through his good arm and squeezed it. 'Give the poor girl the day off, if she wants it!'

Zan's eyes raked Jade's face, studied the tilt of her

chin. Finally his brows shrugged. 'Okay,' he said quietly. 'Okay, okay.'

Somehow, Jade made it out the front door. Her legs were beginning to shake. She started up the hill and then stopped, her eyes widening in dismay. Her house keys! She patted her pockets desperately, but to no avail. They were probably in the living room, by the sofa where she'd found Zan this morning.

She bit her lip. She *couldn't* go back in there. She couldn't! Of course you can, she told herself grimly. You've got to. Taking a deep breath, she set her gear down and turned back to the door.

But no one answered her knock, and she couldn't bring herself to ring the doorbell. If they were upstairs, she didn't want to disturb them. Head bent, she stood there, thinking.

Perhaps they were on the patio. If so, she could hail Zan from the side wall. Jade hurried around the corner and down towards the water.

And they were on the patio, but they were not admiring the view. Zan's muscular back was turned towards her. He stood perfectly straight, blocking Jade's view of Irena, but she could see the blonde's long-nailed fingers spreading out, twining up through his dark gold hair as she pulled his head down to meet her upturned lips. Jade backed around the corner and sagged back against the building.

For this she was going to cancel her plans? Fred's plans? Change the rest of her life? Nausea spiralled through her, followed by a tearing sensation. What had Zan called jealousy? The green-eyed monster, clawing at your guts? He'd said she didn't know that side of love . . . Well, she was learning . . . And he'd forgotten to tell her about the rage . . .

Somehow Jade made it home, somehow she managed to break in by a half-latched window. She packed a bag with a handful of clothes, threw in a randomly-grabbed

book for the bus, found her spare keys. She watered the
plants and left. Newport was too small a town to hold the
three of them. She had to get away. Half an hour later,
she was on a bus, bound north for Boston.

CHAPTER NINE

BUT distance and time offered no solutions to Jade's problems, as she discovered in the next few days. She found refuge with her room-mate from college, as she had known she would. She spent the days wandering the city streets, sketching—and thinking of Zan. She spent the evenings talking with Liz—about Zan. At night she tossed on Liz's couch, alternately thinking and dreaming—of Zan. And three days later, she sat on a bus heading south again, no closer to a solution than ever. But as she'd told Liz, she had to water her plants . . .

Jade adjusted the contoured seat and leaned back, shutting her eyes. What was she going to do? What *could* she do? She couldn't impose on Liz for ever. Couldn't conceive of running to her father in Houston or her mother in California. Wouldn't even contemplate running to Fred. That left Newport . . . the only place in the world she wanted to be right now . . .

She sighed. 'Get him out of your system,' had been Liz's practical advice. 'Spend August in bed with the brute, and you'll probably discover you loathe him . . .' Jade smiled wryly. No doubt that was practical advice, if one happened to be a practical female like Liz. But if you played for keeps . . . She couldn't give herself just for three weeks. Not to Zan. She could give her heart for life, but Zan said she shouldn't be serious . . . Zan didn't want that from her.

She bit her lip. She ought to be running for her life, not returning! Forget the house, forget the plants, forget the signed confession that Zan still held. She half smiled as she thought of that . . . What a farce! What a con job he'd pulled on her with that statement! He would never

162

have sued her, she knew now. It had been one of Zan's jokes, an elaborate bluff to get his way.

But if the threat had been empty, she'd promised all the same. Promised to help him finish a book. What about that? And how was the book coming? she wondered. Had Irena straightened him out?

Her mouth twisted along with her stomach as she thought of the blonde. Think of something else, quick . . . Fred . . . At least she'd taken Liz's advice there, or part of it. 'Take one last look at the guy before you kiss him off. Besides, Dear John letters are cop-outs.' That last bit was good advice anyway. Fred would be home in three weeks, and it was only fair to tell him in person, not to spoil the last of his summer. So she'd written to him, not agreeing to an October wedding, just saying they'd have to talk when he came back. Perhaps that would give him a hint, prepare him a little . . .

She had to stop thinking about all this. Hadn't she packed a book, come to think of it? Groping in the bottom of her overnight bag, she found it, pulled it out, then winced and shut her eyes. It was *The Rookie*, of course. Zan's first book. He was haunting her, that was it. She could run where she wanted, he'd be one step behind, or even closer than that. For Zan was inside her now. Under her skin. She might just as well go back . . .

Sighing, she flipped open the book and read a page at random. She'd read it once already and liked it tremendously, but this time she read it to see Zan, not to follow a plot. Her mouth curved as she read, as she pictured a younger, cockier Zan, a clever golden boy setting out to conquer New York with a typewriter . . . She read another page, then another, then flipped back to the start, missed it and found herself reading the dedication, 'To Al and to Mona.'

And penned in below it, in awkward, left-handed script she'd never seen before, 'and to the darling jade.'

She gasped. When had he written that? It could only have been when she fled to the women's room, that night at the restaurant. And what did it mean? He'd mentioned that in the car, the day they met—something about a quote. No doubt it was a joke of some sort, knowing Zan.

It was late evening, a moonlit, cricket-loud evening, when Jade trudged down her street at last. There would be no foghorns tonight to wake Zan, she thought absently, watching her shadow on the pale sidewalk before her.

Tiny, dark-haired Cathy was sitting on the front steps with the young Navy couple from across the street. In no mood to socialise, Jade waved to her shy, pretty tenant and turned up the side path, fishing her keys out of her jeans.

'Jade!' Cathy hurried behind her. 'Someone was asking for you!' she cried breathlessly. 'A fair man with a broken arm!'

'Oh . . .' Jade groaned. '*Oh*-oh!' She should have expected that—hadn't thought of that in her haste to leave town. 'What did he do?'

Cathy hugged herself nervously. 'He came to the door and asked for you. I told him what you'd asked me to say—that you'd moved away in early June.'

Jade bit her lip. Oh, lord. 'What did he say?'

Cathy shook her head. 'He didn't say anything. He stood there for a moment, very quietly, and then he just pushed open my door—very gently—and walked in. I couldn't stop him!'

'No, of course you couldn't,' Jade breathed. 'Oh, lord, Cathy, I'm sorry! And then?'

'He just strolled through the apartment, looking, then he came back and asked me why I still had some of your plants and furniture. I . . . I could hardly speak by then, but I told you'd let the place furnished, but I didn't know where you were . . . Then he looked at the phone, checking my phone number, I think, then he just walked out again.' She paused for breath.

'Oh, Cathy, I'm *awfully* sorry!' Jade groaned. 'I didn't mean to get you mixed up in my problems.'

'That's okay, Jade,' Cathy assured him. 'But I think you should call the police. Terry said she saw him peeking through your front windows the next day. And your phone's been ringing day and night.'

'Did she see if he walked around back?' Jade asked carefully. If he had, he might have seen her plants in the window. She glanced nervously up the path. Zan on the warpath might not be dangerous, but all the same she'd rather not meet him tonight.

Cathy followed her glance and her eyes rounded. 'She didn't *say*!' she whispered. 'Hadn't you better call the police?'

Jade shook her head firmly. 'It's not that kind of problem, Cathy. Really, it's not. He's not violent.' She rattled her keys briskly and smiled at the girl. 'You've been terrific, Cathy, and thanks very much, and don't worry, okay?'

'Well, if you're sure . . . okay . . .' Looking doubtful, Cathy took the hint, and scurried away.

Flipping on the light, Jade locked the back door behind her and put the chain guard on as well. Her nerves were jumping. Zan was on the warpath for sure; she'd done it now . . . Suddenly, standing in the brightly-lit, curtainless kitchen, Jade felt incredibly exposed. Shivering, she flicked out the lights again. The moonlight washed in through the glass-topped back door and the kitchen window, changing the room to a study in soft greys, pearly whites, velvet-black shadows.

Absently, Jade peeled off her shirt and her bra and stood thinking. He must have wanted to write. He'd be furious! She found her brush and began to brush her hair, soothing her leaping nerves with its soft, flowing crackle. Tomorrow she would either have to apologise, or mail him a cheque for a dictaphone and jump town for good.

Twisting her hair back into a loose knot, Jade wandered to the kitchen sink, turned on the taps and soaped her face. Tomorrow, what was she—above the running water, she heard something heavy move across the back porch.

Eyes shut, she groped wildly for the handles and turned the water off. Heart thumping, ears straining for an alien sound, she froze—then jumped as the door knob rattled.

'Jade? Open up!' Zan's voice sounded utterly uncompromising.

Had he heard the water running? Surely not! Eyes squinched against the soap on her face, Jade stood absolutely still. He wouldn't be able to see her from the door; the counter blocked the view.

'Jade—open this door! I know you're in there.'

He was bluffing; he had to be. Her breath was coming faster now, but he wouldn't hear that.

Something rattled at the lock and Jade nearly opened her eyes. Her housekeys! She'd left them—the door wrenched open, then groaned as it hit the end of the chain. 'Jade, if you want to keep this door, you'd better come open it . . . *Now!*' The low command was more frightening than any raised voice, and Zan sounded unbearably closer now, with the door partly open.

Jade licked suddenly dry lips. She should be angry, not frightened! 'Zan, you stay *out* of here!' she cried passionately.

'Like hell! Open this door!' he demanded.

'No! I don't want—'

The sound of splintering wood cut across her words as the chain end pulled out of the door frame. The door creaked open and his steps sounded loud in the sudden silence.

Chin high and fists clenched, Jade waited. She heard

the hissing intake of his breath as he found her in the leaf-dappled moonlight by the sink, and then slow, advancing footsteps.

'Please . . .' she whispered shakily, her hands lifting blindly to ward him off.

She winced as Zan grabbed the waistband of her jeans, his fingers sliding between the band and her flinching stomach. Hard and warm, his knuckles jabbed into the curve of her belly. 'Zan!' she gasped in outrage as a wave of heat flamed out from the point where he touched her.

'I could wring . . . your . . . neck!' he breathed savagely as he jerked her forward. His tongue licked her left breast, bringing the nipple to throbbing erectness with a single stroke.

'No!' Bending at the waist, Jade arched away from him, realising even as she did that she was presenting her breasts more fully to his lips, rather than escaping them. His ragged breath was almost a growl as he tasted one breast, and then the other.

Her fingers twisted into his thick hair, more to support her shaking legs than to push him away as he arched her back with the pressure of his mouth. 'Zan, please don't,' she whispered, even as she held his head to her breast. She gasped as the soap began to sting her eyes.

His hand dropped her waistband, leaving her clinging blindly to his neck for an instant until his palm cupped her hip, squeezing it as he forced her in to meet his hard thighs. 'Say it . . . like you *mean* it, then . . . Jade,' he muttered bitterly against her flesh as his tongue traced a scorching path from her breast to her throat. His lips lingered there, driving the pulse to a frenzied pace.

'Zan, please . . . my eyes,' she panted as his mouth travelled slowly up the front of her throat and his lips swayed slowly against her.

His teeth closed on her chin in a hungry, nibbling

caress, then his head jerked away. 'Ugh!' he gagged, 'what's that? Soap?'

'Y-yes . . .' she laughed shakily, 'please, can I just wash it off?'

'I don't know,' he mused huskily above her. 'You're pretty docile as is. Maybe I should leave you soaped. Like putting salt on a bird's tail.' His hand squeezed her hip as he spoke and then eased to let her lean back against the sink.

Jade turned in his loosened hold and groped for the cold water. But Zan wasn't going to let her recover that easily. His fingers glided slowly up the front of her thigh, slowed to a hypnotic, tantalising crawl as they climbed the length of her zipper.

Jade shuddered with aching pleasure and splashed icy water into her face. How as she going to stop him? Did she even mean to?

His weight was leaning in steadily to pin her to the sink as he pressed against her hips, and she could feel him harden against her. She sloshed water into her eyes as if she might dive into a wave and escape him, then gasped as his hand cupped her breast.

'Damn you, Jade,' he groaned against the back of her neck. 'It isn't fair! There you are with two breasts, and me with just one hand! I could wring your neck!'

She shuddered convulsively, arching her neck back as his teeth closed in the top of her shoulder. 'Zan, *please!*' she gasped towards the ceiling, and his answering laugh was almost a snarl as he spun her around.

'Please, *nothing!*' he flung out as his mouth came down upon hers and his arm clamped around her waist again. He forced her lips apart with a hunger more savage than tender, deepened the kiss as her mouth trembled and responded, then wrenched his lips away to press them against her throat. 'Why the hell did you run away?' His voice was muffled against her hot skin. 'It was that damned letter, wasn't it? I thought you were in

Greece by now!' His lips brushed across her cheek. 'I've been looking for you ever since Irena left.'

Irena. Jade's eyes widened in outrage as she stared into the dark past his nuzzling, shaggy head. How could she have forgotten Irena? A shudder racked her body from head to foot as Zan's lips took her breast again and his hand slid down inside her jeans to cup her bare hip and pull her closer.

Irena. She'd have thought a few nights with the blonde would have satisfied him for a while. But obviously, once aroused, Zan was not so easily quenched. So Irena had left the fires still burning and he'd come to her to put them out . . .

His mouth came down hungrily over hers again and his arm tightened around her waist as he lifted her off the floor. He was swinging her around towards the mattress.

'Zan, put me *down*!' she stormed. This time, the words were convincing.

Her toes touched the floor and slowly his face lifted above her. 'What?' he murmured dazedly. In the moonlight, his eyes were gleaming-dark, dilated . . . frightening.

'Let *go* of me!' she commanded. She'd used that steely tone a thousand times before in the classroom, but never before on Zan. His lips twisted incredulously even as his arm released her.

She stepped back till her heels hit the mattress and stood staring up at him, her breasts rising and falling as she sucked in air.

'Why?' he asked intensely, his hand stretching out to finger a nipple with dreamlike delicacy as he stared at her face. 'Why stop me, Jade?' he whispered unbelievingly.

'Because I don't *want* you!' she snapped proudly, sweeping his hand aside. Not like this, she didn't want him. Not when she was just a chaser to Irena.

For a moment he stood, absolutely motionless, staring

down at her. Slowly his hand lifted to her throat. Thumb resting in the hollow there, his fingers curled around the back of her slender neck. Her head came up and her eyes widened as she stared at him defiantly. What did he propose to do? Choke her into submission?

Zan's hand squeezed gently and then eased as he looked down at her. 'Your pulse is going crazy,' he murmured thickly. 'Your body wants me, Jade.'

'Well, it's been outvoted,' she retorted crisply, shaking her hair back.

Even in the moonlight, she could see the lines crinkle out from the wide eyes, as his hand traced slowly down to her breast again. His thumb rolled her nipple slowly— a butterfly touch that nearly melted her knees. 'If it's voting we're talking about,' he observed sardonically. 'Have you ever heard of stuffing the ballot box, Jade?' His finger traced a slow, flaming circle around the swollen peak. 'I think I could change your mind.' He was laughing softly, his hand gliding slowly down to her waist and behind it to urge her forward. 'I've got a great write-in candidate.'

'You—go to *hell*,' she said clearly, her eyes blazing. She would *not* be a stand-in for Irena!

His hand dropped away as he looked down at her. His thick brows twitched gently, then stilled. 'I may,' he said thoughtfully, as he turned. Four long steps and he was out the door. It swung gently shut behind him and he was gone.

Jade gaped at the closed door, her body crying for his touch even as she absorbed his departure. She gave a sharp little cry and whirled to find her shirt. She couldn't let him go like that! Not like that. She buttoned the shirt and found her shoes, cursing herself for every kind of a fool as she stumbled towards the door. But when she reached the street, he was gone. The patter of her footsteps matched the sound of her heart as she ran down to the corner. But her anxious eyes found nothing, no long-legged, angry shape striding away in the moon-light. Nothing. Panting, she shook her hair back and peered into the distance. He must be far ahead of her now. Long gone. And angry.

Jade pulled a deep breath of the cool air. And what if she caught him? What if she followed him home? Her apology might start with words, but it wouldn't end with them. Not tonight . . . And why should she apologise for not wanting to be used? she asked herself miserably as she turned back up the street. Why indeed?

CHAPTER TEN

It was midday before Jade found herself at the door of Zan's condominium. All morning she'd sat by a silent phone, cursing herself, cursing him, praying it would ring. But it hadn't. So she would have to make the first move. They still had a book to finish, after all, she told herself firmly.

But that wasn't the real reason she stood here, she admitted as she knocked again. She was here because she couldn't stay away.

'Now isn't that just like a man?' Garden spade in hand, Jerry's fat little wife stood in the next yard, shaking her frizzy blue curls in disgust. 'Didn't your husband tell you he was leaving?'

It took a second to find air to reply. And it wasn't the woman's misconception that had stolen it. 'He . . . 's gone?' Jade croaked.

'And took my hubby with him!' the old lady clucked indignantly. 'They'll probably end up in a ditch somewhere, in that car!'

'Where'd they go, Mrs Connally?' Jade tried to look mildly amused, mildly interested, and failed utterly. And why, oh, why had he gone?

'New York, with my Jerry driving.' Mrs Connally sniffed and knelt cautiously to study the flowerbed before her. 'We'll just have to pray.'

'Did they . . . say when they'd be back?' Jade asked carefully.

Mrs Connally cut out a weed with one short, vicious scoop. 'I'm supposed to collect my old goat at the train station in Kingston tonight. I haven't decided if I'll bother . . .' She looked up suddenly, her wispy eyebrows rising. 'You mean he really didn't tell—'

'I'm sure there's a note inside. Thank you, Mrs Connally!' Jade whipped out her keys and spun away. She was through the door before the old lady spoke again.

Gone. The closing slam of the door seemed to echo through the empty room . . . *Gone*. She leaned back against the door, feeling the emptiness around her gather and press slowly into her lungs. Into her heart.

And *why*? Pushing off of the door, she walked slowly into the room, her eyes sweeping all the places he might have left a note. Oh, why had he gone? Because of last night? Because she wouldn't sleep with him? Oh, *damn* the man! Why couldn't he just . . . just . . . she shook her head hopelessly. Love her, as well as want her? Zan, who said he'd never been in love?

An open envelope and a wad of paper on the kitchen counter caught her eye. The envelope was from Western Union, its end torn open with Zan's usual half-clumsy, half-impatient ruthlessness. The wad of paper was a telegram . . .

What had he said once? That snooping was one way to learn useful facts? She smoothed the paper carefully.

'You win. Mona,' it said. Nothing more. You win . . . what? Jade frowned down at the paper. And when had this come? Yesterday? This morning? Was this why he'd gone? To meet Mona in New York, collect his winnings? Crunching the telegram again, she dropped it back on the counter. And did it really matter? If it wasn't Mona, there was Irena—or the one who liked gardenias, or perhaps he'd take whats-her-name to a foreign flick tonight—*X*-rated, no doubt! She whirled away, her eyes blazing. Well, I just hope you remembered to take your address book, Zan Wykoff, she told him savagely, so you can keep them all straight!

Her eyes widened in horror. Before her, the end table where the manuscript box and the typewriter had lived

all summer was empty. *That* was what he'd taken! . . .
Zan was gone. There was an air of utter finality about
that empty table. He'd taken all that really mattered to
him, hadn't he?

So it was over. She didn't need the note he hadn't
bothered to leave to know that now. The missing manuscript told her. It was over. He'd find some way to work
without her. She smiled bitterly, fighting back the tears.
He hadn't worked so well, *with* her, these last few
weeks, come to think of it . . . Maybe that was the last
and real reason he'd left . . . If Zan needed any reason at
all.

Moving slowly, dreamily, through the empty rooms,
Jade collected her possessions. It seemed to take a long
time, if time was passing at all, to gather them
together—though there wasn't much to take away. A
bamboo brush she'd overlooked, a hairclip, a typed note
Zan had left her once—'Red, gone to see Jerry', and the
plant that he'd said would never share their bed. She
could carry it all in one trip. Eyes wide and distant, she
walked home through the summer dusk, cradling the
begonia. He was gone.

Two figures sat on the front steps as Jade approached the
house. Cathy and a man. She turned down the side path.

'Jade?'

If it didn't last, it wasn't love, she thought dully,
peering up at the thin, handsome face before her. 'Fred,'
she identified him absently. He looked worried.

'Are . . . you all right, honey?' he asked, trying to
take the begonia from her hands.

Studying him, she nodded firmly, and forgot to stop
nodding as she clung to the begonia. His voice was
higher than she'd remembered it. 'Fine, just fine, Fred.
How was Greece?' She backed away down the path and
he followed.

'Jade . . . honey . . . I want to know how it was *here*! I

began to hear rumours—your letters—I had to come back and see if . . .' He searched her face.

Jade took a deep breath. It was so unfair. Zan had spoiled it all. It would never be the same again . . . nothing would . . . 'Fred?' she began.

'What, honey?'

'Come . . . have a cup of tea, and tell me about Greece. And tomorrow, I'll tell you about . . . here . . . Okay?' She bit her lip and looked up at him pleadingly, her eyes wide and swimming.

Fred swallowed and nodded carefully. 'Okay, Jade. I'll go get my suitcase.'

Fred had given up his apartment in May. After all, they'd have returned from Greece married, if all had gone as planned, and he would have lived here. So at the very least, Jade owed him a bed, even if it wasn't the one he'd planned on.

It was Cathy who rescued the situation; Cathy who shyly suggested that Jade could move upstairs to sleep on the fold-out sofa for the rest of the month, while Fred took the first floor apartment. In return for her intrusion, Jade reduced Cathy's rent. It was a simple solution to a painful predicament, and one that would have to do until Fred could find a new apartment. In the meantime, Jade would have to convince him that he would need a place of his own. She'd forgotten his patience.

Fred stared at the ring in his hand, and jiggled it gently. Shaking his head, he held it back out to her. 'Nothing's changed, Jade,' he said firmly.

'I . . .' her breath shook with incredulous, angry laughter, barely suppressed. Was he *that* blind? 'Fred . . . I *can't*. I'm sorry, but I just can't wear it. Don't you see that now?'

The ring before her didn't waver. 'You feel that way now, Jade. I understand. But in a month or two . . .'

She shook her head. 'Fred, I'm sorry, but I won't—'

He picked up her hand, his eyes showing anger for the first time she could ever remember. 'Keep it,' he ordered, dropping it into her palm. 'Let's just not be hasty.'

'Fred, I can't wear it.' She widened her own eyes, trying to force him to understand. Couldn't he see that?

'All right, honey.' He smiled tightly. 'But keep it . . . just in case.'

Jade sighed, defeated. 'Okay, Fred.' There was room in her jewellery box for it, and sooner or later he'd understand. Or at least accept.

Perhaps it was a week later, perhaps a little longer. Time didn't seem to matter much any more. Jade trudged up her street in the dusk. She'd sneaked out before daylight, had walked to that ledge on Ocean Drive that she'd been heading for two months ago at dawn—a lifetime ago—when the whole dreadful mess had started. Like a time-lapse camera, or Monet with his cathedral, she had sat there and painted the beach and the day from sunrise to sunset. Quite possibly, she would never paint another seascape in her life again. Quite possibly she didn't care, either.

Cathy and Fred were sitting on the front porch, and she smiled at them politely. It was good that someone wanted to talk to Fred, to smile for him. Maybe one good thing would come out of all this, after all, if Fred wasn't too blind to see it.

'Jade.' Fred stopped her as she started to walk around him. Cathy hopped up, murmuring some excuse she didn't catch, and fled up the stairs.

'Hi, Fred.' Jade sank down wearily beside him. 'What did you do today?'

He studied her carefully, then sighed. 'I worked on lesson plans, Jade. Something you'd better start thinking about.'

She nodded distantly. Too true. September would be starting some time soon, wouldn't it?

Fred reached out to touch her cheek. 'You're losing weight, honey. You've *got* to snap out of this.'

Jade smiled politely and stood up, reaching for her paint kit.

'Cathy's invited us both to supper tonight,' Fred told her. 'She's made lasagna. We'd better go on up.'

She shook her head quickly, her empty stomach suddenly revolted at the thought of it. 'I don't think I—'

'Jade, you have to eat.'

'I had a sandwich, Fred,' she lied, shaking her head again.

'Jade.' He put a hand on each thin shoulder, holding her. 'I'll make a bargain with you. You eat a good supper, and I'll tell you about a phone call I took for you last night.'

The painting kit broke open as it fell, spilling brushes and tubes of paint around their feet. 'You . . . took a phone call for me?' she repeated.

Avoiding her eyes, Fred crouched to collect the debris. 'Yes. Will you eat supper?'

'*Tell* me, Fred!' She stared down at him, hating him suddenly.

Both hands full, he looked up at her. 'Jade, it wasn't much . . .' Suddenly he looked sorry he'd spoken. 'Will you eat?'

'Yes! *Tell* me!' She knelt in front of him, her eyes wild.

Fred sighed. 'He just said to tell you "hi", and that the book was working at last.'

'That was it?' She searched his face desperately.

His lips tightened. 'He said you should mail the key back, that someone called Mona needed it.' He looked down and found her roll of paintbrushes, tossing them in to the kit. 'I didn't know you had a key . . . You'll come eat now?'

'That was *all*?' Her voice sounded hoarse, she noticed.

'That was all.' Fred reached for the broken top of the kit and stood up. 'So come and eat.'

Somehow she got through the meal. Someone ate the food they put on her plate and it must have been her. Somehow she finally got away, then hurried to a phone booth a few blocks away where she could be alone.

But Zan's phone number had been disconnected. Jade stared at the phone in despair, remembering how he'd once said his apartment was sublet for the summer. Where had Zan been staying then? Was he even still in the city?

There was only one person she could think of to ask, and information did have a number for Irena Adams. It was awfully late to be calling, she thought indifferently, as she dialled. *She's asleep*, she thought as the phone rang again, and then again.

'Hello.' His low, warm voice was unmistakable.

'*Zan.*' Her lips formed his name.

'Hello, hello, hello, hello,' he tried impatiently. 'Come on, speak up or go to bed!'

There was suddenly nothing to say. What a fool she'd been to call! All the numbers she had gathered around her was shredding away at the sound of him.

'Who is it, darling?' Irena's throaty voice carried clearly.

'Some nuisance caller. Want to listen to him listening to you? Hello?' Zan snorted, and the phone clicked down.

So that was that. It's time to put it behind you, Jade told herself, as she wandered homeward. Time to pick up the pieces and start over again. Somehow.

CHAPTER ELEVEN

'YOU'RE sure you won't come with us, Jade? You've always wanted to go to a Tanglewood concert.' Fred looked down at her impatiently as she sat on the top step. 'It would do you good to get away.'

Jade shook her head briefly. 'Thanks, Fred, but . . .'

Cathy sat down beside her, her round eyes anxious. 'You ought to come, Jade! The Berkshire mountains are beautiful, and my parents' house has plenty of room. They'd love to meet you.'

Jade smiled and shook her head briskly. 'Thanks, Cathy, but I've got a week left till classes start. I'm going to wash my hair and do lesson plans. Maybe sleep late tomorrow . . .'

Fred shrugged resignedly. 'Okay, Jade, have it your way. We'll see you late tomorrow, then.'

Cathy's face was a pretty mix of sympathy and delight as she followed Fred to his car, and Jade's eyes were wistful as she watched them drive away. Zan's ill wind had blown someone some good anyway. Another month, and Fred would take that ring back.

Across the street, a Mercedes pulled to a stop and parked deftly. Jade looked down at her hands. Was he working or playing tonight?

'You're Jade.' The slender girl—woman—standing before her had a voice like a bell, clear and light. In daylight her hair would be as silvery as her voice.

Jade's eyes widened. There was no mistaking her. 'And you're Mona,' she said softly.

Mona broke into a delightful grin. 'Zan's long-suffering aunt,' she agreed ruefully.

'*Aunt?*' Jade could feel her jaw dropping.

Mona threw back her head, her laughter tinkling around them. 'You mean the dope still won't admit to that? He's hated that since I was in fourth grade and he was in fifth, and I used to pull rank on him at school!' She sank down on the step beside Jade. 'I've been meaning to come find you for a week, Jade, but Peter and I have been doing such a wholehearted honeymoon, I never got away.' Her eyes, pale, wide, and light grey, crinkled at the corners in a way that was painful to watch.

She was studying Jade now, the cool, shrewd eyes flicking lightly over her face. 'Are you all right, Jade?' she asked suddenly.

Swallowing painfully, Jade nodded and smiled. This doesn't change anything, she told herself desperately.

Mona's silvery, delicate eyebrows disappeared into her bangs, but she nodded. 'You've got to help me, Jade,' she announced.

'Of . . . of course. How?' She couldn't look at those eyes. Couldn't look away. God, it shouldn't hurt like this after three weeks, should it?

'Zan commissioned me last week to buy your wedding gift, and the brute was no help at all!' Mona laughed indignantly. 'I'm supposed to buy you something absolutely exquisite, cost no object, and I haven't got a *clue* as to what you'd like. We're on our way down to Washington tonight—I'm giving Peter a whirlwind tour of the East Coast—and I thought maybe I could find you something there, if you'll give me a hint?'

'I . . . er . . . no. Thank you.' Jade swallowed again.

'No, thank you, what?' Mona asked bluntly, her eyes refusing to release her.

'No, thank you anyway, but I'm not getting married, thanks,' Jade blurted, springing to her feet.

Tilting her head back gracefully, Mona stared up at her. 'Zan was so sure,' she murmured thoughtfully. 'First week in September, he said.'

'He got it wrong. I'm not getting married at all.' She

had to get out of here. Jade took a step backwards.

Still the grey eyes, Zan's eyes, held her. 'I see,' Mona said softly. 'Okay.' She glanced towards the car. 'In that case, I have something for you, Jade. Wait here,' she commanded firmly, waiting for Jade's nod before she scampered back to the Mercedes.

The man at the wheel said something, and Mona's laughter pealed out. She skipped back up the steps. 'I was supposed to put this in with your gift.' She handed Jade a white envelope and backed off a pace.

'I . . . thank you.' Jade stared down at the envelope. 'Goodbye, Mona.'

Her laugh tinkled softly. 'I'll be seeing you, Jade.' Light footsteps pattered across the pavement, and a car door shut.

It was too dark to read on the porch. Jade's legs shook as she climbed the stairs, shook so much that she had to sit at the kitchen table before she could open the letter.

She'd never seen Zan's right-hand writing before, but it was not surprising. It was big, jubilant, fiercely angular. He started off without greeting, as if he were resuming a broken conversation, not beginning one.

'I couldn't find the confession, Jade, but consider the debt cancelled. Paid in full. We were even by the time I'd wrung it out of you, but I couldn't bear to tell you that.

I never told you the quote either, did I? It's nothing much, but I always liked it. I thought I might use it as the title for this book.

It concerns the British J-Boat, *Endeavour*, which just barely missed winning the America's Cup, as you know now. It's by John Scott Hughes.

"Am I sentimental about the old *Endeavour*?" he asks. Why "the darling jade nearly broke my heart!"

Be happy, Zan'

His words were blurring, vanishing behind a curtain of tears. If only she *could* have broken Zan's heart! If only he'd had a heart for the breaking! Jade dropped the letter and groped her way to the bathroom. She stood under the shower, crying, until she couldn't stand any more, then she knelt and cried on. *God*, it had no right to hurt so much any more! Wouldn't it ever stop? Wouldn't she ever be free of him? If love lasted for ever, did the pain last too?

The pain continued, but the hot water finally gave out. Shivering, she crept out of the shower. Numbly, mechanically, she dried herself, combed her hair out and blew it dry. She made a cup of coffee and forgot to drink it. It was time to be gone anyway. There was no way she could stay here tonight, no way she could face a bed and the time to think. Pulling on a light sweater and jeans, she started out of the door, then stopped.

The letter was on the kitchen floor. Gently, carefully, she folded it and slipped it into her pocket. She would never read it again. She would keep it always.

There was no moon tonight, but her feet knew where they were going. Knew it long before she did. Halfway down the hill, Jade looked up to see the lights of the bridge curving across the dark sky, but by then it was too late. Her feet carried her on down the road, across the damp grass, and up to the door.

For a long time she stood there, as if, any moment, Zan would open to her. Finally, sighing, she drifted around the corner to the low wall which enclosed the patio. From here she'd seen Irena and Zan kissing, so long ago. Somehow Irena didn't matter any more. Just Zan, and the great, gaping hole he'd torn in her life when he left it.

Jade sprang up on to the wall and sat there, dreaming. She could almost see him pacing the patio, hear his warm voice spinning out the words, see him pausing at the end of each circuit to stare out at the harbour, his honey-dark hair falling down towards his eyes. She hugged herself violently, shivering, then stepped down on the patio stones.

The curtains were drawn across the glass doors. Jade didn't bother to try the handles; they would be locked, and she felt closer to him out here, anyway. Slowly she padded down the steps to the dock.

The floats echoed hollowly under her pacing feet as she walked out into the harbour. Funny how light it was out here tonight. The lights of the town fanned out across the still water, jewelled and glittering spears reaching towards the cove, flickering and re-forming as a slow-gliding boat cut across them.

Jade sank down on the end of the dock and breathed deeply. This was as close as she could get, unless she went to find him. Her wide eyes followed the arc of white lights beyond the harbour. Over that bridge, and three hours to the south, was that so far? Be happy, he'd said . . . Don't be serious, he'd said too.

Sighing, she lay back to look up at the stars. How about a sign? she pleaded. But the stars stayed fixed, glimmering down just for Newport. None went rocketing southward.

Jade watched until the stars doubled and re-doubled before her swimming eyes, and finally she had to shut them out. Her eyes closed and she lay there while the floats creaked and rocked gently, creaked and rocked.

Her eyes fluttered open and she blinked up at the sky . . . How long had she been asleep? Her body was stiff from the cold and the stars had wheeled across the night. The dipper was not where she'd left it.

The dock echoed hollowly to a footstep. And another.

Jade blinked slowly. She'd dreamed this too often . . . that light, slow, pacing would be striding across her dreams for the rest of her life. She sat up and the ghost steps stopped. The bridge still beckoned southward.

The footsteps came on again. Slow. Heartbreaking.

Carefully, she stood up. How did the myths work? If you turned around to look, your love would be gone? Now she knew why the fools always had to turn.

The footsteps stopped again as she swung around, but Zan was still there, a broad-shouldered, silent shape, the dark head lifting slowly. Slowly, dreamily, they closed the last few feet between them, and they stood staring at each other, silent, unmoving.

'Zan?' she breathed.

His eyes caught the lights and threw them back glittering. 'I didn't think you'd recognise me, without the cast,' he said huskily.

'Zan!'

Between her arms, his waist was hard, warm and trembling. His arms wrapped around her, crushing her against his chest. His chin was rasping across her hair. 'I don't care, I don't care, I don't care!' he whispered savagely.

'Don't care what, Zan?' Her voice was shaking, and his heart was thumping against her ear, echoing the jubilant, thunderous beat of her own.

'I don't care if you think you're getting married tomorrow; I don't care if you don't love me; I don't care if you don't even know *how* to love! You are mine and I'm not letting you go again! Not ever!'

There wasn't enough air in her lungs to laugh with; it came out on a shuddering breath. 'Please *don't*! Oh, *please* don't, Zan. I—'

His lips caught the rest of her words and they clung together, swaying gently as the docks rocked. Finally he closed the kiss, turned his mouth to her eyes, her cheeks, her throat.

'Oh, God, I love you, Zan,' she whispered, arching her neck back beneath his lips.

His mouth froze against her ear. 'Would you repeat that, please?' he asked politely.

'I love you,' she laughed softly.

He leaned his forehead against hers, staring down at her. 'Come again?'

'I love, love, *love* you!' She smiled up at him, then rubbed her nose against the crisp hair at the base of his throat.

His big hand clamped on her chin, pulling her face up to meet his gaze. 'And when the hell did you finally figure *that* out, Jade?' he demanded tautly.

Standing very still, she moved a hand to his chest, felt the heart slamming there. She tried to shake her head, but his fingers prevented it. 'I'm not even sure, now, Zan . . . I suppose the night we went to the restaurant, was the first time I really—'

'Bloody, hopping *hell*! If that's the case, Jade, would you please tell me what you were doing in Freddie's bed two weeks ago, when I tried to phone you?' His hand glided from her chin slowly down her throat and his look was murderous.

'In bed with—I—he said *that*?' she sputtered, thunderstruck.

'I . . . you weren't?' Zan's voice was very quiet, but his head lifted slowly. 'He said you were in bed right there, that you wouldn't come to the phone, and that you two were getting married in—' Jade shook her head urgently. 'I'll kill the bastard!'

He spun away towards land and she caught at his arm with both hands. 'You *can't*, Zan! He's gone!'

Zan turned back again, slowly, his face granite. 'Where?'

She shook her head. 'I'll tell you when you cool down.'

His hands reached absently to grip her shoulders, comb into her hair and follow it up to her temples. 'And I left the thumbscrews in New York,' he sighed ruefully. 'I'll just have to torture it out of you with my bare hands.' He tipped her head back and his mouth covered hers, hungry, urgent, unbelievably tender.

She was panting lightly when his head lifted at last. His hands rubbed her shoulders restlessly, hesitated, and then, in sudden decision, he swung her into his arms.

'Zan!' she gasped.

'Lord, you're cold, sweet,' he said huskily, turning towards the patio. 'How long have you been out here?'

She leaned her head against his shoulder and sighed happily. 'Oh, since nine or ten.'

She could feel his laugh as well as hear it. 'I've been sitting on your doorstep since ten o'clock. Exactly two hours and fifty minutes after Mona called.' He stopped walking to kiss her chin. 'I'd finally decided Mona was wrong. That you were off somewhere, sleeping with Fred or even someone new!'

'Mona called you?'

'Mmhmm.' He stopped to sit on the patio wall, and gathered her closer. 'The girl's no fool. And she had a gambling debt to pay off.'

Jade nodded, remembering the telegram. 'What did you win, Zan?'

He laughed softly and stood up again. 'A long, long-standing bet, sweet.' He looked slowly around the harbour and then down at her again. 'I bet her she'd be married before I was.' He laughed again. 'It was always a sure win!'

He manoeuvred them both carefully through the doorway. 'You've sure got long legs, there, Red.'

'Sorry . . .'

'Hey, no complaints! I love every inch of them.' His lips twitched upwards. 'And plan to.'

Jade laughed delightedly. 'And what were the terms of the bet, Zan? What did you get?'

He stopped at the foot of the stairs, smiling down at her. 'We were in high school when we made it. Things seemed a little simpler back then . . . The winner was to get whatever his heart desired.'

It was hard to tell one heart's beat from the other now,

Jade noticed in passing. 'And that was?' she whispered.

'She gave me my choice tonight between a lifetime supply of butter almond ice cream and you,' he whispered back, a smile tugging at the corners of his lips.

'And you chose?' she laughed up at him.

'You'll find out,' he promised, as he started up the stairs.

Zan paused just inside the bedroom door. His head turned to the wide, pillow-heaped bed and then he looked down at her, his brows a shaggy, enquiring line. Jade's answering smile was serene. Tonight was tonight. If Zan's desire for her ended with the daylight, she would face that tomorrow. But for now—just let it be now.

Reading the answer in her eyes, Zan laid her gently across the bed. 'It's the best view in the house,' he said huskily, staring down at her. Slowly he began to unbutton his shirt, his eyes never leaving her face.

But it had been the wrong thing to say. She thought of Irena and her head turned restlessly, her outflung hair rustling against the spread. The bed rocked and Zan's shoulders arched over her, his arms sliding beneath her. His breath steamed against her skin as his lips stroked down the line of her throat. 'Why did you leave me, Zan?' she whispered, trembling.

His lips paused and his head lifted above her. 'Why?' Against her, his chest heaved with angry, incredulous laughter. 'Jade, I couldn't sleep, I couldn't think, I couldn't write You said you didn't want me, told me to go to hell. What was I supposed to do? Stay around till something snapped and I hurt you some way you'd never forgive?' He shook his head angrily, his hands biting into her shoulders. 'And then, to top it off, Mona's telegram came. There she'd found and won her love at last. And here I was, knowing what I wanted, seeing it slip further and further away each day . . . I couldn't *stand* any more. I had to go.' He sat up restlessly, glaring down at her. His wide eyes had a reckless, determined glint to them as his hands found the bottom edge of her sweater and pulled it up.

'And if you loved me, why didn't you let me know?' he challenged softly.

'You said, that time in the boat—' Jade paused as he pulled the sweater over her head, then she waited till his eyes came back to her face, 'you said that I should play around, that I shouldn't be so serious about love.'

His laugh came out in a single explosive breath. 'Except for *me*, Jade! I didn't want you serious about anyone else, damn right! That's all I meant.

'What else?' he challenged fiercely, his hands sliding slowly up her sides till his thumbs found her breasts. 'What else stopped you?'

She barely had air for the one word. 'Irena.'

Zan nodded once. 'Irena.' His thumbs moved in slow, delicate circles, and he smiled slowly as her eyes widened, and her breath came faster. 'I tried every way I could think of to make you see I wasn't interested in her.' His hands glided slowly to the clasp at the front of her bra. 'That "love affair" she refers to consisted of one night, three years ago. We went to a publisher's cocktail party together, Jade, had lots of free champagne, and I guess I got a little . . . accommodating.' He smiled crookedly, then his smile faded as he saw her breasts. He stroked her with a single, delicate finger, his eyes darkening. 'She's never let me forget it. I suppose she'd like to get her little claws into me . . . fifty per cent of my royalties is better than ten per cent.' His eyebrows twitched in amusement. 'Don't ever mix business and pleasure, Jade. I've been regretting that slip for years, but she's too good an agent to let go.'

He leaned down to kiss her breast gently and with a soft groan, she arched up to meet his mouth. 'Anything else bothering you, sweet?' he murmured against her skin.

Her hands twisted through his hair and held. 'The . . . rest of your . . . address book collection.'

Zan laughed softly. 'And I thought you got those eyes from eating too much spinach!' He kissed his way slowly up to her face and touched noses with her, his eyes enormous and dark. Their eyelashes tangled. 'I've gone through fourteen years' worth of girls looking for you, Jade. We sure got our schedules mixed up somehow.' His mouth brushed tantalisingly across the surface of her lips and then lifted again. 'But there hasn't been anyone else since you crashed into my life.' Grey eyes stared intensely into green. 'And there never will be again.'

She ran her hands slowly up his hard arms, slid them around to trace the muscles of his shoulders and neck. 'But you said you've never been in love . . .'

'Right, nimwit.' The smile was shining through his voice and his eyes began to crinkle. 'I never have—till you.'

His mouth brushed along her cheek, lifted to hover above her mouth. 'That reminds me, Red, which kind of kiss is this—love or lust?' Hot, slow, and hungry, his mouth covered hers. Her lips parted softly and the bed, the world—no, their tangled bodies seemed to be spinning down into warm, dizzy darkness.

Gradually, eyes shut, Jade discovered she could breath again.

'Hmm?' he murmured above her. 'Which?'

'I . . .' she smiled blindly, and managed to shake her head.

'Don't know? . . . let's try the other one.' Zan's voice smiled above her and then they whirled slowly into the darkness again to a cadence of muffled drums.

'Hmm?' he coaxed at last, his quickening breath fanning her cheek.

'. . . can't . . . tell the . . . difference, Zan.'

'*Bright* girl,' he whispered mockingly.

*   *   *

In the last, velvet hour before the dawn they whispered drowsily, their bodies twined together. Beneath her ear, his slow, steady heart-beat was the homiest sound she'd ever heard. 'So where'd you stay?' she murmured lazily, her eyes closed.

Zan's hand stroked her shoulder rhythmically, absently. 'With my ward—Al's son—and his aunt. They've always got a room for me when I need it.' He took a deep, contented breath.

Fingers outstretched, she slid her hand slowly through the crisp, tickling hair across his chest. 'I figured you stayed with Irena.'

She felt him snort silently. 'I was trying to *forget* women, sweet. I didn't need Irena stroppin' round my knees like a hungry cat.' He shifted slightly and pulled her closer, thinking. 'But that's not fair,' he murmured sleepily at last. 'She was a big help. We sat down and brainstormed all one night, tore the manuscript right down to the roots. It was Irena who figured out the problem.'

Jade rubbed her cheek against his skin in silent apology. 'Problem?'

'Mmm. I was writing a love story, not a thriller.' His arm tightened around her. 'Once I stopped fighting that, it went like a shot. It'll be a good book . . . new kind of story for me . . .'

Zan lay quiet for some time, his fingers gliding slowly up and down her back. When he spoke at last, his voice was huskier, rougher than before. 'So you'll quit your job, sweet? Come and be a painter instead of a teacher?' His hand stilled against her skin. 'I believe Winslow Homer liked the Bahamas,' he offered coaxingly.

It was so strange to hear that note of uncertainty in his low voice. 'Twist my arm,' she suggested, mischievously.

'Later,' he promised, the smile back in his voice. 'Or if

that doesn't work, I could always try blackmail . . . I have this confession . . .'

Jade laughed softly. 'I thought you lost that?'

She felt him shake his head. 'No. It's in my wallet.'

'But you said—'

His arm tightened painfully. 'It was all I had of you, Jade. I wasn't about to return it.' His low laugh sounded shaky. 'I'm going to frame it, now.'

She sat up suddenly to stare down at him. 'Don't you *dare*!' She snapped, scowling as she shook a wisp of hair out of her eyes.

'You big enough to stop me?' Zan laughed, sitting up in one smooth surge. 'I bet I could lick you with one hand tied behind my back.' His tongue stroked a moist, fiery trail up her shuddering spine to her shoulder where he bit her gently.

Gasping, she whirled away from his teeth and leaned back against the pillows, her eyes wide and laughing.

Zan sat still, stroking her face and her body with dark, caressing eyes. Jade flushed shyly and looked beyond him. The view was indeed superb, the finest anywhere.

'Red?' Zan asked huskily.

Silently, she smiled and glanced to either side of her, searching for a redhead.

'My darling? Jade?' Zan leaned slowly towards her, his voice rough with sudden urgency.

She leaned forward, hooked an arm around his neck to pull him to her, groaned with soft pleasure at the weight and hardness of him. 'Yes, Master?' she purred contentedly.

'Love me?' A boy as well as a man hid behind the roughness of that low question, and tears burned her eyes. It wasn't for just this moment that he was asking.

Tightening her arms, she breathed the words into his ear, making them a kiss as well as a promise. 'For ever and ever.'

Beyond the shaggy outline of his head, she could see

the bridge, spanning the night sky to link two dark and different shores in a curve of joyous light. 'For ever and ever, love.'